'I was born and learned mine English in Kent, in the Weald, where English is spoken broad and rude.'

— *William Caxton*

Haec super arvorum cultu pecorumque canebam
Et super arboribus, Caesar dum magnus ad altum
Fulminat Euphraten bello:
Carmina qui lusi pastorum, audaxque juventa,
Tityre, te patulae cecini sub tegmine fagi.

Vita Sackville-West

HERITAGE

Futura

A Futura BOOK

First published in Great Britain in 1919 by
William Collins Sons & Co Ltd

First Futura edition 1975
Reprinted 1984

ISBN 0 8600 7086 7

Printed in Great Britain by
The Guernsey Press Company Limited,
Guernsey, Channel Islands.

Futura Publications
A Division of Macdonald & Co (Publishers) Ltd
Maxwell House
74 Worship Street
London EC2A 2EN

A BPCC plc Company

To My Mother

PART I

I

Two years of my life were spent in a rough gray village of the Apennines; a shaggy village, tilted perilously up the side of the hill; a rambling village, too incoherent to form a single perspectived street, but which revolved around, or, rather, above and below, a little piazza warm with present sun, though grim with unknown, conjectured violence in the past. Here stood the massive civic palace, ancient and forbidding, with its tower poised and tremulous in the evening sky; and here the church, with its marble pietà, the work, it was said, of Mino da Fiesole. A mountain torrent poured down the village, a wild little storm of water, brown and white, spanned by a bridge, which rose abruptly to a peak, and as abruptly descended. In the evenings the youth of the village drifted towards the bridge, gossiped there, sang a snatch of song, or indolently fished. In the silent midday, stretched at length on the flat stone parapet, they slept. . . .

The village was called Sampiero della Vigna Vecchia.

If I dwell thus upon its characteristics, it is from lingering affection and melancholy memories. My sentiment is personal; irrelevant to my present purpose. I resume:

In this village – and it is for this reason that the village started up so irrepressibly in my thoughts – I had as a companion a man named Malory. Like me, he was there to study Italian. We were not friends; we lodged in the same house, and a certain degree of intimacy had thereby necessarily forced itself upon us; but we were not friends. I cannot tell you why. No quarrel stood between us. I liked him;

7

I believe he liked me. But we were each conscious that our last day in Sampiero would also be the last day we spent together. No pleasant anticipation of continued friendship in our own country came to sweeten our student days in Italy.

Yet for one week in those two years Malory and I were linked by the thread of a story he told me, sitting out under a clump of stone-pines overlooking the village. It linked us, indeed, not for that week alone, but, though interruptedly and at long intervals, for many years out of our lives. Neither of us foresaw at the time the far-reaching sequel of his confidences. He, when he told me the story, thought that he was telling me a completed thing, an incident revived in its entirety out of the past; I, when I later went to investigate for myself, went with no thought of continuance; and finally, I, when I departed, did so in the belief that the ultimate word was spoken. Our error, I suppose, arose from our delusion that in this affair, which we considered peculiarly our own, we held in some measure the levers of control. Our conceit, I see it now, was absurd. We were dealing with a force capricious, incalculable, surprising, a force that lurked at the roots of nature, baffling alike the onlooker and the subject whose vagaries it prompted.

I should like to explain here that those who look for facts and events as the central points of significance in a tale, will be disappointed. On the other hand, I may fall upon an audience which, like myself, contend that the vitality of human beings is to be judged less by their achievement than by their endeavour, by the force of their emotion rather than by their success; if this is my lot I shall be fortunate. Indeed, my difficulty throughout has been that I laboured with stones too heavy for my strength, and tried to pierce through veils too opaque for my feeble eyes. Little of any moment occurs in my story, yet behind it all I am aware of tremendous forces at work, which none have rightly understood, neither the actors nor the onlookers.

It was less of a story that Malory told me, than a quiet meditative reminiscence, and he wove into it a great deal which, I begin to suspect, as I think over it, without extracting from my granary of words and impressions any very definite image, was little more than the fleeting phantom of his own personality. I could wish that fate had been a little kinder to me in regard to Malory. I am sure now that he was a man in whom I could have rejoiced as a friend.

When I think of him now, he stands for me as the type of the theorist, who, when confronted with realities, strays helplessly from the road. He had theories about love, but he passed love by unseen; theories about humour, but was himself an essentially unhumorous man; theories about friendship between men, but was himself the loneliest being upon earth. At the same time, I sometimes think that he had something akin to greatness in him; a wide horizon, and a generous sweep of mind. But I may be mistaking mere earnestness for force, and in any case I had better let the man speak for himself.

He said to me as we smoked, 'Do you know the Weald of Kent?' and as he spoke he indicated with his pipe stem a broad half-circle, and I had a glimpse of flattened country lying in such a half-circle beneath my view.

His words gave me a strong emotional shock; from those gaunt mountains, that clattering stream, I was suddenly projected into a world of apple-blossom and other delicate things. The mountains vanished; the herd of goats, which moved near us cropping at the scant but faintly aromatic grass of the hill-side, vanished; and in their place stood placid cows, slowly chewing the cud in lush English meadows.

'I fancied once that I would take up farming as a profession,' said Malory. 'I have touched and dropped many occupations in my life,' and I realised then that never before in the now eighteen months of our acquaintance had he made to me a remark even so remotely personal. 'Many occupations, that have all fallen from me, or I from them. I am an inconstant man, knowing that no love can hold me long. Perhaps that is one of the reasons why I have never married. Such people should not marry, or, if they do, should at least choose a partner as inconstant as themselves. When I say inconstant, I mean of course the temperamentally, not the accidentally, inconstant. It is a new kind of eugenics, a sort of moral eugenics.

'So at one period of my life I had a fancy that I would try my hand at farming. I think perhaps it was one of my most successful experiments. I have a great love for the country people; they are to me like the oaks of the land, enduring and indigenous, beautiful with the beauty of strong, deep-rooted things, without intention of change. I love in them the store of country knowledge which they distil as resin from a pine, in natural order, with the revolving seasons. I love the unconsciousness of them, as they move unheeding, bent only on the practical business of their craft. I revere the simplicity of their traditional ideals. Above all, I envy them the balance and the stability of their lives.'

I wasn't very much surprised; I had always thought him a dreamy, sensitive sort of fellow. I said,

'But you surely don't want to change with them?'

Malory smiled.

'Don't I? Well, perhaps I don't. I should have to give up my sense of wonderment, for they have none. They may be poems, but they are not poets. The people among whom I lived were true yeomen; they and their forefathers had held the house and tilled the land for two hundred and fifty years or more, since the Puritan founder of their race had received the grant from, so tradition said, the hands of Cromwell in person. Since the days of that grim Ironside, one son at least in the family had been named Oliver.

'The house was partly built of lath and plaster and partly of that gray stone called Kentish rag, which must have been, I used to reflect with satisfaction, hewn out of the very land on which the house was set. I remembered how the thought pleased me, that no exotic importation had gone to the making of that English, English whole. No brilliant colour in that dun monochrome, save one, of which I will tell you presently. Have patience, for the leisure of those days comes stealing once more over me, when haste was a stranger, and men took upon them the unhurrying calm of their beasts.

'After the fashion of such homes, the house stood back from a narrow lane; a low stone wall formed a kind of fore-court, which was filled with flowers, and a flagged path bordered with lavender lay stretched from the little swing-gate to the door. The steps were rounded with the constant passing of many feet. The eaves were wide, and in them the martins nested year after year; the steep tiled roofs, red-brown with age, and gold-spattered with stonecrops, rose sharply up to the chimney-stacks. You have seen it all a hundred times. Do you know how such houses crouch down into their hollow? So near, so near to the warm earth. Earth! there's nothing like it; lying on it, being close to it, smelling it, and smelling all the country smells as well, not honey-suckle and roses, but the clean, acrid smell of animals, horses, dogs, and cattle, and the smell of ripe fruit, and of cut hay.

'And there's something of the Noah's Ark about a farm; there's Mr Noah, Mrs Noah, and Shem, Ham, and Japhet, and the animals, because there's nothing in the world more like the familiar wooden figures of our childhood than the domestic animals. If you have never seen a cow before, gaunt and unwieldy, what a preposterous beast you would think it. Also a sheep – the living sheep is, if anything,

11

even more like the woolly toy than the woolly toy is like the living sheep. And they all fit in so neatly, so warmly, just like the Noah's Ark. However, I won't labour the point. . . .

'This house of which I am telling you was nearer to the earth than most; it had, in fact, subsided right down into it, sinking from north to south with the settling of the clay, and the resultant appearance of established comfort was greater than I can describe to you. The irregularity of the building was the more apparent by reason of the oak beams, which should have been horizontal, but which actually sloped at a considerable angle. I found, after I had lived there no more than a couple of days, that one adopted this architectural irregularity into one's scheme of life; the furniture was propped up by blocks of wood on the south side, and I learnt not to drop round objects on to my floor, knowing that if I did so they would roll speedily out of reach. For the same reason, all the children of the house, in this generation as no doubt in many generations past, had made their first uncertain steps out in the garden before they climbed the hill or toppled down the incline of their mother's room.

'I paused, on the evening of my arrival, before my future home. I said to myself, here I shall live for one, two, three, possibly four years; how familiar will be that unfamiliar gate; I arrive with curiosity, I shall leave, I hope, with regret. And I foresaw myself leaving, and my eyes travelling yearningly over the house and the little garden, which in a moment the bend of the lane would hide from me for ever. I say for ever, for I would not court the disillusion of returning to a once happy home. Then, as my eyes began to sting with the prophetic sorrow of departure, I remembered that my one, two, three, or possibly four, years were before and not behind me; so, amused at my own sensibility, I pushed open the swing-gate and went in.

12

'The house door opened to my knock. I stood on the threshold – I stand there now in spirit. Have you experienced the thrill of excitement which overcomes one when one stands on the threshold of new friendship, new intimacy? such a thrill as overcame me now as I stood, literally and figuratively, in the doorway of the Pennistans' home. I scanned the faces which were raised towards me, faces which were to me then as masks, or as books written in a language I could not read, but which would speedily become open and speaking; no longer the disguise, but the revelation of the human passion which lay behind. The facts of life at Pennistans' I could foresee, but not the life of the spirit, the mazy windings of mutual relation, the circumstance of individual being. These people were anonymous to me in their spirits as in their names.

'You might fare far before you came upon a better-favoured family. I was in the low, red-tiled kitchen; they were seated at their supper round a central table, the father, the mother, three sons, and the daughter Nancy. Amos Pennistan had the bearing, the gravity, and the beard of an apostle; I never saw a nobler looking man; he had his coat off, and his scarlet braces marked his shirt like a slash of blood. His sons, as they raised their heads to me from their bread and porridge, cast their eyes over my city-bred frame, much as calves in a field raise their heads to stare at the passer-by over the hedge, and I felt myself in the presence of young, indifferent animals.

'An old, old woman was sitting over the fire. No mention of her had been made in our correspondence, nor did I then know who she was. Yet had it not been for her, and for the strange flame she had introduced into this English home, the story I am endeavouring to tell you might never have sprung up out of the grayness of commonplace.

'The faintest smell floated about the room, and as I stood in slight bewilderment looking round I wondered what it

13

could be; it was oddly familiar; it transported me, by one of those sideslips of the brain, away from England, and though the vision was too dim and transitory for me to crystallise it into a definite picture, I dreamed myself for a second in a narrow street between close, towering houses; yoked bullocks were there somewhere, and the clamour of a Latin city. I have gazed at a rainbow, and fancied I caught a violet ribbon between the red and the blue; gazed again, and it was gone; so with my present illusion. Then I saw that the old woman was fingering something by the fire, and in my interest I looked, and made out a row of chestnuts on the rail; one of them cracked and spat, falling on to the hearth, where she retrieved it with the tongs and set it on the rail again to roast.

'The bullock-like sons took no notice of me beyond their first dispassionate glance, but Mrs Pennistan in her buxom, and Amos in his reticent, fashion gave me an hospitable welcome. I was strongly conscious of the taciturn sons, who, after a grudging shuffle – a concession, I suppose, to my quality as a stranger – returned to their meal in uninterested silence. I was abashed by the contempt of the young men. It was a relief to me when one of them pushed aside his bowl and rose, saying, "I'll be seeing to the cattle, father."

'Amos replied, "Ay, do, and see to the window in the hovel; remember it's shaky on the hinge." I had a sudden sense of intimacy: a day, a week, and I too should know the shaky hinge, the abiding place of tools, the peculiarities of the piggery.

'I wandered out. A mist lay over the gentle hills, as the bloom lies on a grape; a great stillness sank over the meadows, and that mellow melancholy of the English autumn floated towards me on the wings of the evening. I felt infinitely at peace. I reflected with a deep satisfaction that no soul in London knew my address. My bank, my solicitors, would be extremely annoyed when they discovered

14

that they had mislaid me. To me there was a certain satisfaction in that thought also.'

'On the following morning,' continued Malory, 'I rose early. I went out. The freshness of this Kentish morning was a thing new to me. The ground, the air, were wet with dew; gossamer was over all the grass and hedges, shreds of gossamer linking bramble to bramble, perfect spiders' webs of gossamer, and a veil of gossamer seemed to hang between the earth and the sun. The grass in the field was gray with wet. A darker trail across it showed me where the cattle had passed, as though some phantom sweeper had swept with a giant broom against the pile of a velvet carpet. The peculiar light of sunrise still clung about the land.'

For a moment Malory ceased speaking, and the goats, the barren mountains, the impetuous torrent, rushed again into my vision like a wrong magic-lantern slide thrown suddenly, and in error, upon the screen. Then as his voice resumed I saw once more the hedges, the clump of oaks, and the darker trail where the cattle had passed across the field.

'I was at a loss,' said Malory, 'to know how to employ my morning, and regretted my stipulation that my training should not begin until the following day. I wished for a pitchfork in my hand, that I might carry the crisp bracken for bedding into the empty stalls. I heard somewhere a girl's voice singing; the voice, I later discovered, of Nancy, upraised in a then popular song which began, "Oh, I do love to be beside the sea-side," and so often subsequently did I hear this song that it is for ever associated in my mind with Nancy. I could hear somewhere also the clank of harness, and presently one of the sons came from the stable, sitting sideways upon a great shire horse and followed by two other horses; they passed me by with the heavy, swinging gait of elephants, out into the lane where they disappeared, leaving me to my loneliness. I felt that the great fat ball of

15

the world was rolling, rolling in the limpidity of the morning, and that I alone had given no helping push.

'I wandered, stepping gingerly upon the cobble stones, round the corner of the farm buildings, and there, in a doorway, I came unexpectedly upon a girl I had not previously seen. She stood with a wooden yoke across her shoulders, and her hands upon the two pendent buckets of milk. I felt myself – do not misunderstand me – suddenly and poignantly conscious of her sex. The blue linen dress she wore clung unashamedly to every curve of her young and boyish figure, and around the sleeves the sweat had stained the linen to a widening circle of darker blue. Swarthy as a gipsy, I saw her instinctively as a mother, with a child in her arms, and other children clinging about her skirts.'

I thought I understood Malory, a lyre whose neurotic treble alone had hitherto responded to the playing of his dilettantism, with the chords of the bass suddenly stirred and awakened.

'You have probably known in your life one or more of those impressions so powerful as to amount to emotions, an impression such as I received now, as, at a loss for words, this girl and I stood facing one another. I knew, I *knew*,' said Malory, looking earnestly at me as though driving his meaning by force of suggestion into my brain, 'that here stood one for whom lay in wait no ordinary destiny. She might be common, she might be, probably was, rude and uncultivated, nevertheless something in her past was preparing a formidable something for her future.'

As he spoke I thought that, by the look on his face, he was again receiving what he described as an impression so powerful as to amount to an emotion. And he communicated this emotion to me, so that I felt his prophecy to be a true one, and that his story would henceforward cease to be a mere story and would become a simple unwinding off the spool of inevitable truth.

He went on,

'Our silence of course couldn't endure for ever. The girl herself seemed conscious of this, for a smile, not unfriendly, came to her lips, and she said quite simply,—

' "How you startled me! Good-morning."

' "I am very sorry," I said. "Can't I make up for it by carrying those buckets for you?"

' "Oh, they're nothing with the yoke," she answered.

'Here old Amos came round the corner, walking clumsily on the cobbles with his hob-nailed boots. He looked surprised to find me standing with the dairymaid, a little group of two.

' "Morning!" he cried very heartily to me. "You're out betimes. Fine day, sir, fine day, fine day. Well, my girl, done with the cows?"

' "I'm on my way to the dairy, dad," she said.

'I asked if I might come with her.

' "Ay, go with Ruth," said Amos, "she'll show you round," and he went off, evidently glad to have shifted the responsibility of my morning's entertainment.

'Ruth refused to let me carry the buckets, and by the time we reached the dairy – one of the pleasantest places I ever was in, clean and bright as a yacht – their weight had brought a warm flush of colour to her cheeks. Great flat pans of milk stood on gray slate slabs, covered over with filmy butter-muslin; in one corner was fixed a sink, and in another corner a machine which I learnt was called the separator.

' "Father's very proud of this," said my companion, "none of the other farms round here have got one."

'I sat on the central table watching her as she moved about her business; she didn't take very much notice of me, and I was at liberty to observe her, noting her practised efficiency in handling the pans and cans of milk; noting, too, her dark, un-English beauty, un-English not so much, as you might think, owing to the swarthiness of her complexion, as

17

to something subtly tender in the curve of her features and the swell of her forearm. She hummed to herself as she worked. I asked her whether the evening did not find her weary.

'"One's glad to get to bed," she said in a matter-of-fact tone, adding, "but it's all right unless one's queer."

'"Can't you take a day off, being on your father's farm?"

'"Beasts have to be fed, queer or no queer," she replied.

'The milk was now ready in shining cans, and going to the door she shouted,—

'"Sid!"

'A voice calling in answer was followed by one of the sons. Neither brother nor sister spoke, while the young man trundled away the cans successively; I heard them bumping on the cobbles, and bumping more loudly as, presumably, he lifted them into a cart. Ruth had turned to wiping up the dairy.

'"Where is he going with the cans?" I asked.

'"Milk round," she answered laconically.

'That was the first time I saw her,' he added. 'The second time was in full midday, and she was gleaning in a stubble-field; yes; her name was Ruth, and she was gleaning. She moved by stages across the field, throwing out her long wooden rake to its farthest extent and drawing it back to her until she had gathered sufficient strands into a heap, when, laying down the rake, she bound the corn against her thigh, rapidly and skilfully into a sheaf. The occupation seemed wholly suitable. Although her head was not covered by a coloured handkerchief, but hidden by a linen sunbonnet, she reminded me of the peasant-women labouring in the fields of other lands than ours. I do not know whether, in the light of my present wisdom, I exaggerate the impression of those early days. I think that perhaps at first, imbued as I was with the idea of the completely English character of my surroundings, I remained insensible to the flaw which presently became so self-evident in the harmony of my preconceived picture.

'Tiny things occurred, which I noted at the time and cast aside on the scrap-heap of my observation, and which later I retrieved and strung together in their coherent order. As who should come upon the pieces of a child's puzzle strewn here and there upon his path.

'Ruth, my instructress and companion, I saw going about her work without haste, almost without interest. She was kind to the animals in her care after an indifferent, sleepy fashion, more from habit and upbringing than from a natural benevolence. She brought no enthusiasm to any of her undertakings. Her tasks were performed conscientiously, but by rote. Yet one day, when the sheep-dog happened to be in her path, I saw her kick out at it in the belly with sudden and unbridled vehemence.

'I was first really startled by the appearance of Rawdon Westmacott. In the big, shadowy, draughty barn I was cutting chaff for the horses, while Ruth sat near by on a truss of straw, trying to mend a bridle-strap with string. I had then been at Pennistans' about a week. The wide doors of the barn were open, letting in a great square of dust-moted sunlight, and in this square a score of Leghorn hens and cockerels moved picking at the scattered chaff, daintily prinking on their spindly feet, snowy white and coral crested. A shadow fell across the floor. Ruth and I raised our heads. A young man leant against the side of the door, a tall young man in riding breeches, with a dull red stock twisted round his throat, smacking at his leathern gaiters with a riding whip he held in his hand. The rein was over his arm, and his horse, lowering his head, snuffed breezily at the chaff blown out into the yard.

'"You're back, then?" said Ruth.

'"Ay," said the young man, looking suspiciously at me,

19

and I caught the slightest jerk of the head and interrogative crinkle of the forehead by which he required an explanation.

' "This is my cousin, Rawdon Westmacott, Mr Malory," Ruth said.

'The young man flicked his whip up to his cap, and then dismissed me from his interest.

' "Coming out, Ruth?" he asked.

'She pouted her indecision.

' "You shall have a ride," he suggested.

' "No, thanks."

' "Well, walk a bit of the way home with me, anyhow."

' "I don't know that I'm so very keen."

' "Oh, come on, Ruthie, after I've ridden straight over here to see you; thrown my bag into the house, and come straight away to you, without a look into one single thing at home."

' "It'd be better for things if you did look into them a bit more, Rawdon."

'Overcome by the perversity of women, he said again,—

' "Come on, Ruthie."

'She rose slowly, and, untying the apron of sacking which she wore over her skirt, she stepped out into the sunshine. For a flash I saw them standing there together, and I saw Rawdon Westmacott as he ever after appeared to me: a Bedouin in corduroy, with a thin, fierce face, the grace of an antelope, and the wildness of a hawk; a creature captured either in the desert or from the woods. Strange product for the English countryside! Then they were gone, and the horse, turning, followed the tug on the rein.

'I date from that moment my awakening to a state of affairs less simple than I had imagined. I saw Ruth again with Westmacott, and learnt with a little shock that here

20

was not merely an idle, rural, or cousinly flirtation. The man's blood was crazy for her.

'And so I became aware of the existence of some element I could not reconcile with my surroundings, some unseen presence which would jerk me away abruptly to the sensation that I was in the midst of a foreign encampment; was it Biblical? was it Arab? troubled was I and puzzled; I tried to dismiss the fancy, but it returned; I even appealed to various of the Pennistans for enlightenment, but they stared at me blankly.

'Yes, I tried to dismiss it, and to brush aside the haze of mystery as one brushes aside the smoke of a cigarette. And I could not succeed. How trivial, how easily ignored are facts, when one's quarrel is with the enigma of force at the heart of things! It isn't often in this civilised life of ours that one comes into contact with it; one's business lies mostly with men and women whose whole system of philosophy is inimical to natural, inconvenient impulse. It obeys us as a rule, like a tame lion doing its tricks for the lion-tamer. A terrifying thought truly, that we are shut up for life in a cage with a wild beast that may at any moment throw off its docility to leap upon us! We taunt it, we provoke it, we tweak its tail, we take every advantage of its forbearance; then when the day comes for it to turn on us, we cry out, and try to get away into a corner. At least let us do it the honour to recognise its roar of warning, as I did then, though I was as surprised and disquieted as I dare say you would have been, at meeting a living lion in the woods of Kent.

'I could compare it to many other things, but principally I think I felt it as a ghost that peeped out at me from over innocent shoulders. Am I mixing my metaphors? You see, it was so vague, so elusive, that it seemed to combine all the bogeys of one's childhood. Something we don't understand; that is what frightens us, from the child alone in the dark to the old man picking at the sheets on his deathbed. Perhaps you think I am exaggerating. Certainly my apprehension was a very indefinite one, at most it was a dim vision of possibilities unnamed, it wasn't even a sense of the imminence of crisis, much less the imminence of tragedy. And yet . . . I don't know. I still believe that tragedy was there somewhere, perhaps only on the horizon, and that the merest chance alone served to avert it. Perhaps it wasn't entirely averted. One never knows; one only sees with one's clumsy eyes. One sees the dead body, but never the dead soul. The whole story is, to me, unsatisfactory; I often wonder whether there is a conclusion somewhere, that either I have missed, or that hasn't yet been published by the greatest of story-tellers.

'Anyway, all this is too fanciful, and I have inadvertently wandered into an inner circle of speculation, I mean soul-speculation, when I really meant to be concerned with the outer circle only.

'I could lay my hand on nothing more definite than the appearance, certainly unusual, of Ruth or of Westmacott; other trifles were so absurd that I scorned to dwell on them in my mind, the red braces of Amos and that faint scent of roasting chestnuts in the kitchen under the hands of Amos's grandmother. Whenever I went into the kitchen I met that scent, and heard the indefinite mumble of the old woman's toothless mouth, and the smell of the chestnuts floated out, too, into the narrow entrance-passage and up the steep stairs which led to the rooms above. I associate it always now with a narrow passage, rather dark; sloping ceilings; and rooms where the pictures could be hung on the south wall only, because of the crookedness of the house. In the parlour, which balanced the kitchen, but was never used, was an old-fashioned oil-painting of a soldier with whiskers and a tightly-buttoned uniform, and this painting swung out from the north wall and a space of perhaps six inches between the wall and the bottom of the frame.'

22

II

On the morrow we again took our pipes to the clump of pines, and Malory began, in his drowsy, meditative voice, to tell his story from where he had left off.

'I hope you are by now as curious as I was to discover the secret of the Pennistan quality. The family were evidently unconscious that there was any secret to discover. They thought no more of themselves than they did of their blue surrounding hills, though in relation to the weather they considered their blue hills a good deal, and Amos taught me one evening that too great a clearness was not to be desired; the row of poplars over towards Penshurst should be slightly obscured, misty; and if it was so, and if the haze hung over Crowborough Beacon, I might safely leave the yearling calves out in the field all night. I should look also for a heavy dew upon the ground, which would predict a fine day besides bringing out the mushrooms.

'We were standing in the cross-roads, where the white finger-post said, "Edenbridge, Leigh, Cowden," and Amos had corrected my pronunciation from Lee to Lye, and from *Cow*den to Cow*den*. I know no greater joy than returning to the heart of a beloved country by road, and seeing the names on the finger-posts change from the unfamiliar to the familiar, passing through stages of acquaintance to friendship, and from friendship into intimacy. Half the secret of love lies in intimacy, whereby love gains in tenderness what it loses in mystery, and is not the poorer by the bargain.

'Mrs Pennistan came out to join us, and I took the opportunity of asking her whether I might use a certain cupboard for my clothes, as I was pressed for room. She replied,—

' "Granny had that cupboard, but she's surely past using

23

it now, so anything of hers you find in it, hang out over the banister, and I'll pack it away in a box."

'Out of this little material circumstance I obtained my explanation; I went in, leaving husband and wife strolling in the road, for it was Sunday evening, and on their Sunday evening they clung to their hour of leisure. I went in, past the chestnuts, up the stairs, and at the top of the stairs I opened the cupboard door, and explored with my hand to discover whether the recess was empty. It was not, so I fetched my candle in its blue tin candlestick, and lifted out the garments one by one; they were three in number.

'I carried them carefully into my room, with no intention of examining them, but as I laid them on the bed their texture and fashion arrested me. A smell came from them, faded and far away. I held them up one by one: a heavily fringed shawl of Spanish make, a black shirt with many flounces, a tiny satin bodice that would barely, I thought, fit a child. As I unrolled this last, something fell from it: a pair of old, pink shoes, tiny shoes, heelless shoes, — the shoes of a ballet dancer.

'As I turned over these relics I heard some one moving in the passage below, and going to the top of the stairs I called to Ruth. She came up, then seeing the shoes in my hands she gave an exclamation of surprise.

' "Are these yours?" I asked.

' "Mine! no; why, look here," and she held a shoe against her foot, which, although small, outstripped the shoe in width and length. "They're granny's, I reckon," she added.

'Then she took up the bodice and examined it critically.

' "It's a bit rotten, of course," she remarked, pulling cautiously at the stuff, "but where'd you buy satin now to last as well as that? and bought abroad, too."

'The subtlest inflection of resentment was in her tone.

' "Here, give them to me," she said ."Granny can't want these old rags messing up the house. There's little enough cupboard room anyhow. I'll put the shawl away up in the attic, for there's wear in it yet, but the rest can go on the midden."

'I detained her.

' "Tell me first, how comes your grandmother to have these things?"

'She was surprised at my ignorance.

' "To start with, she's father's grandmother, not mine. She's so old, I forget her mostly. . . . She's ninety-six, ninety-seven come Christmas. We're wondering if she'll last to a hundred."

'How callous she was! Triply callous, I thought, because of her own youth, because of her great-grandmother's extreme age, and because of the natural philosophic indifference of her class towards life and death.

' "She was a dancer, once, you know," she went on. "Used to dance on the stage, and my great-grandfather found her there, and married her. What a tiny little thing she must have been, just look at this," and she held the little bodice across her own breast with a gay laugh, like a child trying to put on the clothes of its biggest doll.

'Then she held the skirt against her slender hips to show me how short it was, and pointed her foot in an instinctive dance position.

'She was holding up the bodice by tucking it under her chin. I looked at her, and she blushed, and convinced me that no woman ever stands altogether innocent of coquetry before any man.

' "Tell me more about your grandmother," I said.

' "It's so long ago," she replied. "She had two children, and one was my father's father, and the other was Rawdon Westmacott's mother. You know my cousin Rawdon?"

' "I know him," I said. 'So you and he are of different generations, though there's not more than twelve years between you in age."

25

' "Yes, that's so. Now I come to think of it, there's the old book in the parlour you might like to read, a diary or something, kept by my great-grandfather. It's only an old thing; I've never looked on it myself, but I've heard father talk of it. Shall I get it for you?"

'I begged that she would do so, and she ran downstairs, and returned with a little tartan-covered volume in her hand.

' "Father sets great store by it,' she said hesitatingly, as she gave it up to me.

' "He won't object to my reading it?"

' "Oh, no, if you've a mind."

'She evidently looked down on me a good deal for my interest in the old-fashioned volume.

'Left alone, I drew my chair near to the chest of drawers, whereon I had set the blue candlestick; I had two hours before me, and I felt as an explorer might feel on the verge of a new country. Here was a document written by a dead hand, an intimate document, private property, not edited and re-edited, but quietly owned by dignified and unassuming descendants, who would neither cheapen nor profane by giving the dead man's confidence to the world. It was probable that no intelligently interested eyes but mine would ever read it. I hesitated for an appreciable time before I opened the diary, and in that pause my eyes wandered from the little book to the little garments on the bed, and I fancied that these inanimate objects, made animate by the spirit of their respective owners, called to one another yearningly across the silence of my room.

'When I at last opened the diary I found myself carried straight away into an unanticipated world. The man, whose name and rank, "Oliver Pennistan, captain, Dragoons," I read on the fly-leaf, was writing in Spain. His first entry was dated Madrid, 1830. He wrote without conscious art, and indeed his daily jottings seemed to me solely the occupation of a lonely evening; at one moment he was annoyed because he had been given *pan de municion*, which was hard, black, and uneatable, instead of *pan de candeal*; at another, he had been overcharged by his landlord, and feared he must exchange into a different posada.

'He was innocent of literary artifice, this Pepys of nineteenth century Spain, yet the natural, matter of fact, unstudied candour of his daily biography brought the preposterous age before me, crimped and grotesque, the Spain of Goya. Eighteen-thirty, an incredible period in any country, attained in Spain an incredibility which turned it into a caricature of itself. Oliver Pennistan, I knew, wore whiskers and an eye-glass; tight, straight, high military trousers; drawled; guffawed; said "Egad". As for the women of his acquaintance, I knew them to be frizzed and fuzzed, with faces mauve beneath their powder, and hearts sick with sentiment beneath their tight bodices. I did not know what had taken Oliver Pennistan to Spain, but I supposed that he was a younger son, as I had heard Amos boast of the dozen boys of his grandfather's generation.

'Still I did not connect his Spanish experiences with the Pennistans I knew. I read the Madrid portion of his diary without impatience, because I was greatly entertained by the subtle flavour of the age which I found therein, but when he came to packing his valise preparatory for a trip to Cadiz, I fluttered the pages over, looking for his return to England. I wanted to get to the dancer who now sat in the room below mine roasting chestnuts over the fire. I was disappointed to see that the diary never accompanied him to England, and I began to fear that his courtship and marriage would not be revealed to me.

' "Leaving Madrid with regret," ran the diary, "but have the benefit of agreeable society on the road. Hope to cover thirty miles to the day. I have a broad sash to keep off the colic, and an amulet from a fair friend to keep off the *evil eye*."

27

'Thus equipped, the dragoon rode to Cadiz, and I must do him the justice to say that he looked on the country he rode through with an appreciative eye, noting the scent of the orange-blossom which assailed him as he entered Andalusia, and the grandeur of the rocky passes which connect northern and southern Spain. At the same time, he kept that nice sense of proportion by which tolerable food and lodging remains more important to the traveller than beauty of scenery. He noted also the superior attactions of the Andalusian women, "little, and dark, and for the most part fat, but with twinkling eyes and a smile more *friendly*, if also more *covert*, than their sisters of Madrid."

'I turned over the pages again at this point, and chanced at last upon a phrase which convinced me that he had met his love. Then the book fell from my hand, and I lost myself in a reverie, working my way laboriously through a maze of preconception to the fact that this dancer of whom I had heard from Ruth was not an English dancer, but a Spanish dancer, and as this fact broke like daylight upon me I realised that I had bored into the heart of my mystery. Moments of revelation are intrinsically dramatic things, when a new knowledge, irrevocable, undisputable, comes to dwell in the mind. All previous habitants have to readjust themselves to make room for the stranger. A great shuffling and stampeding took place now in my brain, but I found that, far from experiencing discomfort or difficulty in accommodating themselves to their new conditions, my prejudices jumped briskly round, and presented themselves in their true shape beneath the searching glare of the revelation.

'I read on eagerly, the shadow of disappointment lifting from me. Oliver Pennistan lodged at an inn which provided him with excellent Valdepeñas; his business in Cadiz was somehow connected with wine, and many technical jottings followed, put in as a guide to his memory; I did not understand all his abbreviations, but was nevertheless impressed by his knowledge of sherry. His business took him most of the day. In the evenings he was a free man, and spent his time in the theatre; probably it was here that he first saw his dancer, for at about this time her name began to appear in the diary: 'To the fight with Concha," or "With Concha to the merry-go-round." There were also references to the "Egyptians", who were Concha's people, and the Goya world of Madrid was replaced by a society of Bohemians – bull fighters, mountebanks, acrobats, hunchbacks, thieves, fortune tellers, all the riff-raff of the gipsy quarter.

'I took this as a miniature allegory, for in the Prado at Madrid the Goya portraits of ladies and the Royal family hang upstairs, while in the basement, typical of the underworld into which Oliver Pennistan had now plunged, hang his series of extraordinary cartoons, caricatures, nightmares, peopled with obscene dwarfs and monstrous parasites.

'How remote the England of his boyhood must have seemed to him, his eleven brothers, the hills, the hawthorn, the farm-buildings; if he saw them at all, it must have been as at the end of a long avenue. I looked up, out of my window across the sleeping fields, and returned again to the pages yet hot and quivering with life, written in an ill-lighted posada at Cadiz.

'In the same way that, without a descriptive word, he had contrived to give me an unmistakable impression of the Spain of his day, he now gave me a portrait of the dancer, passionate but strangely chaste, scornful of men, but yielding her heart to him while she withheld her body. He gave me a picture also of his own love, flaming suddenly out of a night of indifference, overwhelming him and sweeping aside his reason, determining him to make a wife of the gipsy he would more naturally have desired as a passing love. I was intimate with his intention, yet he never departed from his catalogue of facts and doings; stay, once he departed from it to say, "Her head sleek as a berry, her little teeth white

29

as nuts." His one description. . . . I looked across at the little silent heap of garments on my bed, that had clasped the fragile being he revered with so much tenderness.

' "To the bull-ring with Concha," he noted on one occasion. "Not to the spectacle, but to the driving in from the corral. Miura bulls, black and small, but agile more than most. They are driven in through the streets in the small hours of morning, together with the tame cattle, by men on horses. These men wear the bolero and high, peaked hat, and carry a long pole armed with an iron point. I would have ridden, but she dissuaded me. We waited on a balcony above a yard. A long wait, but not dreary in such company. There is much *shouting* when the bulls come, and the yard beneath is filled with fury and bellowing; I would not willingly chance my skin among such angry *monsters*, but their drivers with skill manoeuvre each bull by himself into a separate cell where he is to remain without food or drink until morning. A diverting spectacle, had it not been for the press and the stench of ordures."

'I have seen that dim yard myself,' said Malory, 'chaotic with lashings and tramplings, and pawings and snortings, and the vast animals butt against the woodwork, and their huge forms move confusedly in the limited space. Like Pennistan, I would not care to chance my skin. Concha, who being a Spaniard was bred up to violence, was even a little frightened, "clung to me," said the diary, "and besought me not to leave her. We saw the bulls in their cells from above, by the light of torches. These brands may be thrust down to burn and singe and further enrage the beast," but Oliver Pennistan, who had been nurtured on this mild farm among pampered and kindly kine, did not like the sport, so turned away with Concha on his arm and passed through a door into the upper gallery of the arena.

'The vast circle seemed yet vaster by reason of its emptiness. Its ten thousand seats curved round in tiers and tiers and tiers, a gigantic funnel, open to the sky in which sailed a full and placid moon. The arena, ready raked and scattered with whitish sand, gleamed palely below, as if it had been the reflection of the heavenly moon in a pool of water. The great place lay in haunted silence.

'It was here, sitting in a box, that they came to their final agreement. The diary naturally giving me no hint of the words that passed between them, I had to be content with a laconic entry some few days later: "Married this morning at the church of S. Pedro." I sat on in my room wondering what Oliver Pennistan had made of that surrendered, inviolate soul, the no doubt rather stupid and affected soldier, the scion of English yeoman; I wonder what he made of his wildling, sprung as she was from God knows what parentage; the Moorish Empire and the Holy Land had both surely gone to her making. They roamed Spain together for their honeymoon, and I accompanied them in spirit, seeing her dance, not in public places only, but in their room, for his eyes alone, his hungry love her sweetest applause; dancing in her little shift, and teaching his clumsy hands to clap and his lips to cry "Olé!" I wonder too what the mountebanks of the trade thought of Concha's husband, who sat through her performance in the hot, boarded theatres of Spanish provincial towns, and would allow no other man near his wife, and who, when one evening she for pure mischief eluded him, only grieved in silence and thought her love was going from him. I wonder most of all what Concha thought of him, his staid insularity, his perpetual talk of home, and his unassailable prejudices?

'As I came to the last pages of the diary, which ended abruptly on the last day of the year in Valladolid, Ruth knocked on my door and said she had come for the clothes. I was so full of the illuminating romance that I pressed her with questions. She was not so much reserved as merely indifferent, but looking at her warm young face in the uncertain candlelight I knew that therein, rather than in her speech, lay the answer to all my queries. I had seen the portraits of Amos Pennistan's father, and of Rawdon Westmacott's mother, daguerrotypes which hung, enlarged, on either side of the kitchen dresser, and I knew that in that generation no sign of the Spanish strain had appeared. I looked again at Ruth, at her sleek brown head, her glowing skin, her disdainful poise; looked, and was enlightened. I urged her memory. Could she recall no anecdote, dear to her father when in a mood of comfortable expansion, a family legend of her grandfather's youth? Yes, she remembered hearing that the children had an uneasy time of it, blows and kisses distributed alternately between them, now hugged to their mother's breast, now sent reeling across the room. . . . She had been gay, it seemed, that ancient woman, deliciously gay, light-hearted, generous, full of song, but of sudden and uncertain temper. But she remembered, though it was not worth the telling, that Mrs Oliver Pennistan, in her sunniest mood, would set her children on hassocks to watch her, their backs against the wall, would take down her hair, which was long and a source of pride to her as to all Spanish women, would take her shawl from the cupboard, and, stripping off her shoes and stockings, would dance for her children, up and down, the sinuous intricacies of an Andalusian dance. I wondered what Oliver Pennistan thought, when, coming in of an evening with the mud from the turnip fields heavy on his boots, he found his wife with hair and fingers flying, dancing to the music of her own voice on the tiled floor of his ancestral kitchen?'

III

'Now,' said Malory, 'I scarcely know how to continue my story. I have told you how I went to live with the Pennistans, and I have told you Oliver Pennistan's Spanish adventure, and the rest lies largely in hours so full of work that no day could drag, but which in words would take five minutes' reproducing. I have told you already how I loved that simple monotone of life. I had arrived in autumn, an unwise choice for a novice less enthusiastic than myself, for soon the trees were bare of the fruit which had so rejoiced me, bare, too, of the summer leaf, and the working day, which at first had drawn itself out in long, warm, melting evening, now rushed into darkness before work was done, and not into darkness alone, but into chill and wet, so that you might often have seen me going about my work in the cowsheds with a sack over my shoulders and a hurricane lantern in my hand. I do not pretend that I enjoyed these squally winter nights. They had the effect of dulling my perception, and presently I found myself like the country people whose life I shared, considering the weather merely in its relation to myself; was it wet? then I should be wet; was it a bright, fine day? then I should be dry. My standpoint veered slowly round, like the needle of a compass, from the subjective to the objective. I wish I could say as much for many of my contemporaries. Then in our age as in all great ages, we might find more men living, not merely thinking, their lives.'

In after years I remembered Malory's words, and wondered whether he had found on the battlefield sufficient signs of the activity he desired.

'I remember how entranced I was,' he went on, altering his tone, 'by the sense of ritual in the labouring year. I thought of the country as a vast cathedral, teeming with worshippers, all passing in unison from ceremony to ceremony as the months revolved. When I had come to join the congregation, apse and column and nave were rich with fruit, the common fruit of the English countryside, plum and apple, damson and pear, curved and coloured and glowing with the quality of jewels; then busy hands came, and packed and stored the harvest into bins, and colour went from the place, and it grew dark. A long pause full of meditation fell. The trees slept, men worked quickly and silently, no more than was imperative, and from darkened corners spread the gleam of fires which they had lighted for their warmth and comfort. But then, oh! then the place was suddenly full of young living things, and of a light like pearls; children laughed, and over the ground swept a tide which left it starred with flowers, and a song arose, full of laughter and the ripple of brooks. The spring had come.'

He was strangely exalted. I knew that my presence was forgotten.

'The shepherd and his nymph were not long lacking in this Arcadian world. I met them crossing the fields, I spied them beneath the hedges, I learned to step loudly before entering the dairy with my pails of milk. I loved them, more perhaps as a part of the picture than for their own sakes. To me they were Daphnis and Chloe, not the gamekeeper's son and the farmer's daughter.

'The match was favourably viewed by Amos Pennistan, though Nancy was but eighteen and her lover two years older. I was honoured by an invitation to the wedding. I had already woven a little tale for myself around those country nuptials, a celebration which, although slightly irregular, would have become my lovers better than the parochial gentility which did actually attend their union. I had pictured them by a brook, Daphnis in, to our minds, becomingly inadequate clothing, Chloe's muslin supplemented by chains

34

of meadow flowers such as the children weave, accompanied by their flocks and the many young creatures, lambs, kids, and calves, as are characteristic of that least virginal of seasons. No wooing; no; or if there must be wooing, let it be sudden and primitive, and of the nature of a revelation, and let the oak trees be their roof that night, and the stars the witnesses of their natural and candid passion. But passion, poor soul! was put into stays and stockings, had his mad gallop checked into a walk, while fingers poked, eyes peeped, and tongues clacked round the prisoner. Alas for the secret of Daphnis and Chloe; shorn of the dignity of secrecy, it glared in the printed column, was brayed out from the pulpit, was totted up in pounds and shillings. Food entered to play his hospitable and clumsy part. For days Mrs Pennistan baked, roasted, and kneaded cakes and pastries, and daily as she did it her temper disimproved. Such beauty as was Chloe's, the beauty of health and artlessness, was devastated by the atrocious trappings of respectability. . . .

'What a commonplace tale! you will say, and a vulgar one into the bargain! and indeed you will be right, if a miracle can become a commonplace through frequent working, and if you look upon the marriage of two young creatures as a social convenience, ordained, as we are told, for the procreation of lawful children. I have told you nothing but the love of rustic clowns. But as the great words of language, life and death, love and hate, sin, birth, war, bread and wine, are short and simple, and as the great classical emotions are direct and without complexity, so my rustic clowns are classical and enduring, because Adam and Eve, Daphnis and Chloe, Dick and Nancy, are no more than interchangeable names throughout the ages.

'My Arcady missed its lovers. I realised after they had gone that they had been real lovers, imperative to one another, and that they had not simply drifted into marriage as

a result of upbringing and propinquity. Had their parents'
consent been for some reason refused, they would, I am
convinced, have gone away together. Amos Pennistan, in
one of his rare moments of expansion, told me as much
himself. "Nancy," he said, "it never did to cross Nancy.
She was strong-willed from three months upward. Ruth,
now, she's a steady, tractable girl for all her dark looks. Of
the two, give me Ruth as a daughter."

'You may imagine my profound interest in the study of
this strain sprung from the stock of Concha and Oliver Pennistan. Here I had Nancy, with her slight English prettiness,
and the fiery will which might never be crossed; and Ruth,
who looked like a gipsy and was in fact steady and tractable. I could not help feeling that fate had her hand on
these people, and mocked and pushed them hither and
thither in the thin disguise of heredity. You remember
Francis Galton and the waltzing mice, how he took the common mouse and the waltzing mouse, and mated them, and
how among their progeny there were a common mouse, a
black and white mouse, and a mouse that waltzed; and
how in the subsequent generations the common brown house
mouse predominated, but every now and then there came
a mouse that waltzed and waltzed, restless and tormented,
until in the endless pursuit of its tail it died, dazed, blinded,
perplexed, by the relentless fate that had it in grip. Well,
I had my mice in a cage, and Concha, the dancer, the
waltzing mouse, sat mumbling by the fire.'

I shuddered. I did not understand Malory. He had spoken
of the violence of his feeling when he first caught sight of
Ruth; I could not reconcile that mood with his present chill
analysis.

'You held a microscope over their emotions,' I said.

'I was afraid there would not be many emotions left now
that Nancy was gone,' he replied regretfully. 'I missed her
as a study, and I missed her as an intrinsic part of my

Arcady. I turned naturally for compensation to Ruth and to Rawdon Westmacott, but here I realised at once that I must dissociate the figures from the landscape. They would not fit. No; contrive and compress them as I might, they would not fit. I am very sensitive to the relation of the picture to the frame, and I was troubled by their southern exuberance in the midst of English hay and cornfields. Now could I but have had them here . . .' and again the cropping goats, the mountains, and the torrent rushed across the magic lantern screen in my mind.

'I told you that I knew young Westmacott was there crazy for her; he had no reserve about his desire, but hung round the farm with a straw between his teeth, his whip smacking viciously at his riding-boots, and his eyes perpetually following the girl at her work. He would look at her with a hunger that was indecent. Me he considered with a dislike that amused while it annoyed me. I often left my work when I saw him looming up morosely in the distance, but old Amos dropped me a hint, very gently, in his magnificently grand manner, after which I no longer felt at liberty to leave the two alone. If they wanted private interviews they must arrange them when they knew my work would take me elsewhere.

'I was not sorry, for I had no affection for Westmacott, and it amused me to watch Ruth's manner towards him. I had heard of a woman treating a man like a dog, but I had never seen an expression put into practice as I now saw Ruth put this expression into practice towards her cousin. She seemed to have absolute confidence in her power over him. When it did not suit her to notice his presence, she utterly ignored him, busied her tongue with singing and her hands with the affair of the moment, never casting so much as a glance in his direction, never asking so much as his help with her work; and he would wait, lounging against the doorway or against a tree, silent, devouring her with that hungry look in his eyes. Often I have seen him wait in vain, returning at last to his home without a word from her to carry with him. His farm suffered from his continual absence, but he did not seem to care. And she? did she get much satisfaction out of her ill-treatment of his devotion? I never knew, for she never alluded to him, but I can only suppose that, in the devilish, inexplicable way of women, she did. In his presence she was certainly an altered being; all her gentleness and her undoubted sweetness left her, and she became hard, contemptuous, almost impudent. I disliked her at such moments; self-confidence was unbecoming to her.

'Then, when she wanted him, she would whistle him up like a little puppy, and this also I disliked, because Westmacott, whatever his faults, wasn't that sort of man, and it offended me to witness the slight put upon his dignity. He didn't seem to resent it himself, but came always, obedient to her call. And he would do the most extraordinary things at her bidding. Mrs Pennistan told me one day that when the pair were children, or, rather, when Ruth was a child of ten and he was a young man of twenty-two, she would order him to perform the wildest feats of danger and difficulty.

'"And he'd do what she told him, what's more," said Mrs Pennistan, to whom these reminiscences were obviously a source of delight and pride, as though she, poor honest woman, shone a little with the reflected glory of her daughter's ten-year-old ascendancy over the daring young man. "Lord, you would have laughed to see her standing there, stamping her little foot, and defying him to go down Bailey's Hill on his bicycle without any brakes, and him doing it, with that twist in the road and all. . . . One day she wanted him to jump into the pond with all his clothes on, and when he wouldn't do that she got into such a rage, and stalked away, and wouldn't speak to him, enough to make a cat laugh," and Mrs Pennistan with a great chuckle doubled herself up, rubbing her fat hands in enjoyment up and down her thighs, straightening herself again to say, "Oh, comical!" and to wipe her eye with the corner of her apron.

'"Well, now I declare!" she said suddenly, craning her neck to see over the hedge. "If she isn't at her old tricks again!"

'I followed her with a thrill to a gap in the hedge whither she had darted – if any one so portly may be said to dart. There, across the field, by the gate, stood the pair we had been discussing, and I was actually surprised to find that the little ten-year-old girl whom I had half expected to see was a well-grown and extremely good-looking young woman. She was sitting on the gate, and Westmacott was lounging in his usual attitude beside her; even at that distance his singular grace was apparent.

'They seemed to be looking at the two carthorses which were grazing, loose in the field.

'"She's up to something, you mark my words," said Mrs Pennistan to me.

'I agreed with her. Ruth was pointing, and the imperious tones of her voice floated across to us in the still evening; Rawdon was following the direction of her finger, and now and then he turned in his languid, easy way that covered – with how thin a veneer! – the fierceness beneath, to say something to his companion. I saw his hand drop the switch he carried, and fall upon her knee. Her manner became more wilful, more imperative; had she been standing on the ground, she would have stamped. I heard Rawdon laugh at her, but that seemed to make her angry, and with a resigned shrug he pushed himself away from the gate and began to walk across the field.

'"Lord sakes," said Mrs Pennistan anxiously, "whatever is he going to do?"

'I begged her to keep quiet, because I wanted to see any fun that might be going.

'Mrs Pennistan was not happy; she grunted.

'Ruth was perched on the gate, watching her cousin. I was delighted to have an opportunity of observing them when they thought themselves alone. Besides, I intensely wanted to see what Rawdon was going to do. He walked up to one of the horses, hand outstretched and fingers moving invitingly, but the horse snorted, threw up its head, and cantered lumberingly away to another part of the field. Rawdon followed it, pulling a wisp of grass by means of which he enticed the great clumsy beast until he was able, after some stroking and patting, to lay his hand upon its mane. Ruth, on the gate, clapped her hands and called out gaily.—

' "Now up with you!"

' "Lord sakes!" said Mrs Pennistan again.

'I saw Westmacott getting ready to spring; he was agile as a cat, and with a leap and a good hold on the mane he hoisted himself on to the horse's back. The horse galloped madly round the field, but Westmacott sat him easily – not a very wonderful feat for a farm-trained boy to accomplish. As he passed Ruth he waved his hand to her.

'She wasn't satisfied yet; she called out something, and, the horse having come to a standstill, I saw Rawdon cautiously turning himself round till he sat with his face to the tail. Then he drummed with his heels to put the horse once more into its lumbering gallop.

'I saw the scene as something barbaric, or, rather, as something that ought to have been barbaric and only succeeded in being grotesque. Ruth ought to have been, of course, an Arab girl daring her lover in the desert to feats of horsemanship upon a slim unbroken thoroughbred colt. Instead of that, Westmacott was just making himself look rather ridiculous upon a cart-horse. But the intention was there; yes, by Jove! it was; the intention, the instinct; he was wooing her in a way an English suitor wouldn't have chosen,

40

nor an English girl have approved. Mrs Pennistan, however, saw the matter in a different light, as a foolish and unbecoming escapade on the part of her daughter; so, thrusting herself between the loose staves of the fence and waving her hands angrily, she called out to Westmacott to have done with his dangerous nonsense.

'He slipped off the horse's back, and Ruth slipped down off the gate, the man looking annoyed, and, in a slight degree, sheepish, the girl perfectly self-possessed. Mrs Pennistan rated them both. Westmacott kicked sulkily at the toe of one boot with the heel of the other. I glanced at Ruth. She had her hands in the big pockets of her apron and was looking away into the sky, with her lips pursed for an inaudible whistle. Her mother stormed at her.

' "You're getting too old for such nonsense. It was all very well when you were a chit with pig-tails down your back. And you, Rawdon, I should ha' thought you'd ha' known better. What'd Pennistan say if he knew of your larking with his horses? I've a good mind to tell him."

' "I've done the brute no harm," he muttered.

' "Well, I'll tell him next time, see if I don't. What did you do it for, anyway?"

' "A bit of fun . . ." he muttered again, and, his smouldering eyes resting resentfully upon her, he added something about Ruth.

'Ruth brought her gaze slowly down from the clouds to bend it upon her cousin. Their eyes met in that furnace of passion and hatred with which I was to become so familiar.

' "Ay, Ruth told me," stormed Ruth's mother. "An old tale. You let Ruth alone and she'll let you alone, and we'll all be better pleased. Now be off with you, Rawdon, and you, Ruth, come in to your tea."

'Her excitement had grown as it beat in vain against the rock of Ruth's indifference.

'Ruth,' said Malory after a long pause, and paused again.

'She is a problem by which I am still baffled. I do not know how to speak of her, lest you should misunderstand me. That first impression of which I have already told you never wore off. Do not think that I was in love with her. I was not. I am not that sort of man. But I was always conscious of her, and I cannot imagine the man who, seeing her, would not be conscious of her.

'She on her part was, I am certain, unaware of the effect she produced. Before I had been very long on the farm I had come to the conclusion that she was a slow, gentle, rather stupid girl, obedient to her parents in all things, less from the virtue of obedience than from her natural apathy. She and I were thrown a good deal together by reason of my work. I tried to draw her into conversation, but no sooner had I enticed her, however laboriously, into the regions of speculation than she dragged me back into the regions of fact. "Ruth," I would say, "does a woman cling more to her children or to her husband?" and she would stare at me and reply, "What things you do say, Mr Malory! and if you'll excuse me I have the dairy to wash down yet."

'I am a lover of experiments by nature, and having no aptitude for science it is necessarily with human elements that I conjure in my crucible. You said I held a microscope over emotions. I say, rather, that I hold my subject, my human being, like a piece of cut glass in the sunlight, and let the colours play varyingly through the facets.

'Sunday afternoon was our holiday on the farm, and to the worker alone a holiday is passionately precious. It is all a matter of contrast. On Sunday afternoon I would take Ruth for a walk; the sheep-dog came with us, and we would go through shaw and spinney and young coppice, and along high-hedged lanes. One spot I loved, called Baker's Rough, where the trees and undergrowth had been cleared, and wild flowers had consequently gathered in their millions: anemones, wood-violets, bluebells, cuckoo-flowers, primroses, and later the wild strawberry, and later still the scarlet hips of the briar. I never saw a piece of ground so starred. Here we often passed, and we would climb the hill-ridge behind, and look down over the Weald, and fancy that we could see as far as Romney Marsh, where Rye and Winchelsea keep guard over the melancholy waste like little foreign towns. We stood over the Weald, seeing both fair weather and foul in the wide sweep of sky; there a storm, and there a patch of sun on the squares of meadow. On fine days great pillows of white cloud drifted across the blue, painted by a bold artist in generous sweeps on a broad canvas, and those great clouds were repeated below in the great rounded cushions of trees. We looked over perhaps fifty miles of country, yet scarcely one house could we distinguish, but when we looked for a long time we made out, here and there, a roof or an oast-house, and I used to think that, like certain animals, these dwellings had taken on the colour of the land. For the most part, a clump of trees would be our nearest land-mark.

'I could evoke for you many of those hours when, with the girl beside me, I explored the recesses of that tender country. Without sharing my enthusiasm, she was yet singularly companionable, happy and contented wherever our footsteps led us, with the reposeful quality of content essential to a true comrade.'

He was silent, and I considered him covertly as he sat hugging his knees and staring into the distance with a faraway look on his face. He was, I thought, a queer chap; queer, lonely, alien; intensely, damnably analytical. As I watched him, his head moved slightly, in a distressed, unconscious manner, and his brow contracted into a frown that emphasised the slight negative movement of the head. Yet he did not share his difficulties with me. He dismissed them with a sigh, and a gesture of the hand, and resumed,—

'I mentioned just now the place called Baker's Rough.

Ruth came to me one morning with glowing eyes.

' "There's flowers such as you never saw on Baker's Rough to-day," she said mysteriously.

'I tried to guess: mulleins? ragged robins? periwinkles? but it was none of those. She would not tell me. I must come and see for myself.

'We set out after tea for Baker's Rough, walking quickly, for we had only an hour to spare. As we drew near, the sheep-dog, who had run on ahead, set up a tremendous barking at the gate. I cried,—

' "Gipsies!"

'There was a real gipsy encampment, caravans hung with shining pots and pans, gaudy washing strung out on a line, a camp fire, lean dogs, curly-headed children. Ruth had guessed aright when she guessed that I would be pleased. Amos hated gipsies, but I loved them. I've never outgrown the love of gipsies that lurks in every boy. Have you?'

His eyes were actually sparkling as he asked the question, and I was overcome by a feeling of guilt. Often I had thought this man a prig. He was not one, but simply an odd compound of philosopher and vagrant, poet and child. I resolved not to be hard on him again. I was uncomfortably suspicious that it was I who had been the prig.

'As we stood looking,' he went on, 'a woman came down the steps of a caravan, and, seeing us, invited us with a flashing smile to come into the camp. Ruth was delighted; she followed the woman, looking like a gipsy herself, I thought, and the children came round her, little impudent beggars, staring up into her face and even touching her clothes. She only laughed, curiously at home; I felt, despite my love of the roaming people, over-educated and sophisticated. I was loving the camp self-consciously, almost voluntarily, aware that I was loving it and rather pleased with myself for doing so.'

'Your mind twists,' I interrupted, 'like the point of a corkscrew.'

He laughed, but he looked a little hurt, taken aback, checked on his course.

'I am sorry,' he said, 'you are right to snub me for it. Well, Ruth at any rate was thoroughly at home, and I could see that the gipsy was sizing her up with her shrewd eyes, and wondering whether I should be good for half-a-crown or only a shilling.

'She let Ruth sit on a stool and stir the pot over the fire; it smelt very good, though it probably contained rabbits, which of all foods in the world is the one I most dislike. Then she offered, inevitably, to tell our fortunes, and Ruth, as inevitably, accepted with alacrity. She stretched out her little brown hand, strong and hard with work.

'Of course the gipsy told her a lot of nonsense, and I stood by, acutely apprehensive that I should be drawn in an embarrassing rôle into the prognostications. I had come there with Ruth; therefore, in the gipsy's eyes, I must be Ruth's young man. I took off my cap to let the gipsy see that my hair was going gray on the temples. But it wasn't any use; I found myself appearing as the middle-aged man whose heart was younger than his years, and who would finally carry off the young lady as his bride.

'I tried, of course, to laugh it off, but to my surprise I saw Ruth growing very red and her mouth quivering, so I told the gipsy we had heard enough and that we had no more time to spare. Ruth rose, the pleasure all died away from her face. Then, to add to the misfortunes of the evening, I heard a scream and an outburst of laughter from a neighbouring caravan, and, looking round, I saw Rawdon Westmacott jump to the ground in pursuit of a young gipsy woman, whom he caught in his arms and kissed.

'I looked hastily at Ruth; she had seen the thing happen. The distress which had troubled her face gave way to anger;

45

the name "Rawdon!" slipped in involuntary indignation from her lips. Then an instinct asserted itself to pretend that she had seen nothing, and to get out of the place before her cousin had discovered her. But she conquered the instinct, staring at Westmacott till he turned as though compelled in her direction.

'Not a word did they speak to one another then, but in the silence her anger and contempt flashed across at him like a heliograph, and his vexation flashed back at her. She stood there staring at him deliberately, staring him out of countenance. God! how vexed and furious he was! It makes me laugh now to remember it. I never knew what a fool a man could look when he was caught red-handed. The gipsy only giggled vulgarly, and tried to rearrange her tumbled dress. Ruth never even glanced at her, and presently she removed her gaze, from Westmacott – it seemed quite a long time though I suppose it was not really more than a few seconds – and turned to me.

' "Shall we go?" she said.

'We went, Ruth haughty, and I at a loss for words. Decidedly the expedition had not been a success. The sheep-dog ran on in front and tactfully barked, and in throwing little stones at him relations were re-established between us. I was prepared not to allude to the incident, but Ruth was bolder; she grappled directly with the difficulty.

' "You saw Rawdon?" she said with suppressed violence.

' "I . . . Well, yes, I saw him."

' "What was he doing there? He was up to no good with those gipsy women."

'I had nothing to say; I knew she was right.

' "He's always after women,' she added violently.

'I knew that she would not have said this to me had she not been completely startled out of her self-control.

' "He cares for you though, in his heart," I said, rather inanely.

46

' "Does he!" she exclaimed. "It doesn't look like it."

' "Well," I said, "he rides the cart-horses bare-back with his face to their tails to please you."

' "Oh, you may joke," she said; "he wants to please me now, but where'd I be if I belonged to him? He'd sing a very different song."

' "It rests with you, after all," I ventured.

'She was silent, swishing at the hedges with her stick as she passed.

' "Doesn't it?" I urged.

' "Oh – I suppose so."

' "How do you mean, you suppose so? Nobody wants you to marry him; your parents don't; your brothers don't. You need never see him again. Send him away!"

' "I can't do that," she said in a very low voice.

' "Why not?"

' "I can't . . . I sometimes feel I can't escape Rawdon," she cried out. "He's always been there since I can remember, I think he always will be there. There's something between us; it may be fancy; but there's something between us."

' "Hush!" I said, startled as I was; "here he is."

'He caught us up, walking rapidly, and I could see at a glance that he was determined to have it out with Ruth in spite of my presence. He came up with us, and he took her by the arm.

' "Ruth!" he said, in a vibrant voice. "I want a word with you. You've misjudged me."

'We had all come to a standstill.

' "I can't misjudge what I see," she answered very coldly.

' "You saw, you saw! well, and what of it? That was only a bit of fun. Damn you, if you treated me a bit better yourself . . ."

' "Let me alone, Rawdon," she said, shaking him off. "You can do as you like, that's your affair, only let me alone. I don't want to talk to you. You go your way, and I'll go mine."

'"Your way!" she said, scowling at me. "Your way's my way, as you'll learn."

'"Now don't you come bullying me, Rawdon," she said, but I think she was frightened.

'"Well, you speak me fair and I won't bully you. I was up to no harm, only larking around. . . . Come, Ruthie, haven't you a smile for me? You treat me cruel bad most days, you know, and I don't take offence. Ruthie!"

'"We're not alone, Rawdon," she said sharply.

'I thought he muttered, "No, damn it!" between his teeth, and just then I felt a hand close over my wrist on the side farthest from Westmacott, a little imploring hand that checked in the nick of time my impulse to move away. She spoke bravely, as though the contact gave her courage.

'"That'll do, now, Rawdon, don't come making a scene. There's nothing to make a scene about."

'"But you'll not sulk me?" he said.

'"I'll not sulk you, why should I?"

'"Then give me a kiss, for peace."

'"Let me be, Rawdon."

'She was troubled, now that her anger had passed. I would have walked on, but for the dry, fevered fingers gripping my wrist.

'A new idea had taken possession of Rawdon's mind; his eyes glowed in the noble, architectural carving of his face, that so belied the coarseness of his nature.

'"I'm your cousin, Ruth!" he cried satirically.

'He caught her by the shoulder and turned her towards him. I thought she would have struggled, and indeed I saw the preparatory tautening of her frame; then to my astonishment she yielded suddenly, flexible and abandoned, and he kissed her regardless of my presence; kissed her ferociously, and pushed her from him.

' "I'll see you to-morrow?" he asked.

' "To-morrow, likely," she answered indifferently, with a quick return to her old contemptuous manner.

'He nodded, put his hand on the top bar of the adjoining gate, and vaulted it, walking off rapidly across the fields in the direction of his own farm.

' "And let me tell you," said Ruth, as though she were continuing an uninterrupted conversation, "he'll be back around that gipsy place to-night as sure as geese at Michaelmas. He's as false as can be, is Rawdon."

' "Then I think you were weak with him," I said. "Are you afraid of him?"

"It's like this," said Ruth, with that great uneasy heave of the uneducated when confronted with the explanation of a problem beyond the scope of their vocabulary, "we never get straight, Rawdon and I. He cringes to me, and then I bully him; or else he bullies me, and then I cringe to him. But quarrel as we may, we always come together again. It's no good," she said with a note of despair in her expressive voice like the melancholy of a violin, "we can't get away from one another. We always come together again."

'I was sad; I foresaw that those two would drift into marriage from pure physical need, though there might well be more hatred than love between them.

'In the meantime I tried, not always very successfully, to keep Ruth away from him; she liked being with me, I know, and I think she even welcomed a barrier between herself and her all-too compelling cousin, and so it came about that our Sunday afternoons were, as I have told you, usually spent together. There were times when she broke away from me, when the physical craving became, I suppose, too strong for her, and she would go back to Rawdon. But for the most part she would come after dinner on Sundays, silent and reserved, to see if I was disposed for a walk. She would come in her daily untidiness, with the colour blowing in her cheeks, as beautiful and as wild as a flower. I used to feel sorry for Westmacott and his hot blood.

'On these afternoons I tried my experiments on Ruth, and I sometimes wonder whether she ever caught me at the game, for she would give me a scared, distrustful glance, and turn her head away. She was curiously lazy for so hard a worker, and in sudden indolence she would refuse to move, but would lie on the ground idle and half asleep, and would do nothing but eat the sweets I gave her. I never saw a book in her hand. Once,' said Malory, throwing a bit of wood at the goats, 'I thought I would convert her to Art. I brought out some treasured books, and showed her the pictures; she was neither bewildered, nor bored, nor impressed, nor puzzled; she simply thought the masterpieces unspeakably funny. She laughed. . . . I was absurdly offended at first, then I began to come round to her point of view, and now I am not at all sure that I don't agree. She opened out for me a new attitude.

'After the failure of my pictures, I tried her with a more tangible object. I took her to Penshurst. In telling you of this I am making a very real sacrifice of my pride and self-respect, for, as sometimes happens, I have realised since, from my disinclination to dwell in my own mind upon the incident, that the little rapier of humiliation went deeper than I thought, down to that point in the heart where indifference ceases and essentials begin.'

As Malory said this, he looked at me with his quizzical, interrogative expression, as if to see how I was taking it. I noticed then that he had a crooked smile which gave to his face a quaint attraction. He was a clean-shaven man, with lean features and a dark skin; graying hair; I supposed him to be in the neighbourhood of forty.

'When I asked Ruth if she would come to Penshurst with

me,' he continued, 'she said she must change her dress. She was absent for about half an hour, while I waited in the garden and threw stones for the sheep-dog. When she joined me I saw that she had done her best to smarten herself up; she had frizzed her hair and put on a hat, and her blouse was decorated with some sort of lace – I can't give you a closer description than that. I scarcely recognised her, and though I felt that I was expected to make some comment I knew at the same time that I was physically unable to do so. 'How nice you look!'' were the words that my will hammered out in my brain, but the words that left my lips were, "Come along."

'We started thus unpropitiously, and the strain between us was tautened at every step by the mood of excitement which possessed her. I had never known her like this before. Usually she was quiet, lazy about her speech, and not particularly apposite when she did make a remark, yet I had always found her a satisfactory companion. To-day she chattered volubly, and the painful conviction grew upon me that she was trying to be coy; she hinted that she had broken an appointment with Westmacott; I became more and more silent and miserable. I had anticipated with so much pleasure our going to Penshurst, and I knew now that the afternoon was to be a failure. When we reached the house, bad became worse; Ruth giggled in the rooms, and the housekeeper looked severely at her. She made terrible jokes about the pictures; giggled again, crammed her handkerchief against her mouth; pinched my arm. At last my endurance gave out, and I said, "We had better go home," and I thanked the housekeeper, and said we would find our own way out.

'Ruth was very crestfallen as we went silently across the park; she walked with hanging head beside me, and as I looked down on the top of her absurd hat I was almost sorry for her, but I was really annoyed, and childishly dis-

51

appointed, so I said nothing, and stared gloomily in front of me. I thought that if I thus marked my disapproval of her sudden mood she would never repeat the experiment, and that next day she would return to her blue linen dress and her habitual reserve. I did not think she would make a scene, but rather that she would be glad to pass over the disaster in silence.

'I was surprised when she stopped abruptly.

' "I suppose you'll never take me out again?" she said, as though the idea had been boiling wildly in her brain till it found a safety valve in her lips.

' "My dear Ruth . . ." I began.

' "How cold you are!" she cried violently, and she stamped her foot upon the ground. "Why don't you get angry with me? shake me? abuse me? at any rate, say something. Only "my dear Ruth." I suppose I'm not good enough for you to speak to. If that's it, say so. I'll go home a different way. What have I done? What's wrong? What have I done?"

'I realised that she was in the grip of an emotion she could not control. Such emotions came over one but seldom in ordinary life, but when they come they are uncontrollable, for they spring from that point in the heart, which I was speaking of, where indifference ceases and essentials begin. Still, while realising this, I hardened myself against her.

' "Nothing," I said, adding, "except failed to be yourself."

' "What do you want me to be?" she asked, staring at me.

' "My dear Ruth," I said, "I like you in blue linen."

'I swear I only meant it symbolically; it was perhaps foolish of me to think she would understand. She went on staring at me for a moment, then a change came over her face, a wounded look, horrible to see, and I felt I had hurt a child, most grievously, but before I could rush into the breach I had made and build it up again with fair words, she had dropped her face into her hands and I saw that her shoulders were shaking. She uttered no word of reproach or self-justification, no plea; thereby increasing her pathos a hundredfold.

'I was distressed and embarrassed beyond measure; I hated myself, but no longer hated her. I had begun to like her again in the brief period of her rage, and now in the period of her despair I liked her again completely. I implored her to stop crying, and I tried confusedly to explain my meaning.

'She would have none of my explanations, but turned on me cheeks flaming with a shame which forbade any allusion to her clothes. I could see that she was trembling from head to foot, and by the force of her authority over me I gauged the force of her emotion over herself. Genius and passion are alike compelling. Here was a Ruth I did not know, but it was a Ruth I had desired to see, and I triumphed secretly for having divined her under the Ruth of every day.

'Well,' said Malory, 'I have made my confession now, for it partakes of the nature of confession. I never saw that piteous finery again, and I never saw the mood that matched it. She calmed down at length, and we made a compact of friendship, but if ever the name of Penshurst arose in conversation I saw the scarlet flags fluttering in her cheeks.

'Meanwhile the familiarity of the place grew on me, as I had foreseen, and there were many inmates of the farm, now old-established, whom I had known since their birth; plants and animals alike. We were haymaking, a common enough pursuit, but to me full of delight; I loved the ready fields, the unceasing whirr and rattle of the cutter, the browning grass as it lay where it had fallen, and the rough wooden rake in my hand. I loved the curve of the fields over the hill, and the ridges of hay stretching away like furrows. Above all I loved the great stack, which swallowed up the cartloads one by one, and the green tarpaulins furled above it, which made it look like a galleon with sails and rigging.

'I told you I had dipped into many things; I worked once on a Greek trader which plied with figs and oranges from Smyrna to Corinth through the islands of the Aegean. It was a bulky, mediaeval-looking vessel, with vast red sails, very little changed, I should imagine, from the one in which Ulysses sailed on his immortal journey. I learnt a certain amount about the orange trade, but I learnt another thing from that Greek ship which I value more: I learnt about colour, hot, tawny colour, that ran the gamut from the bronze limbs of the crew, through the Venetian sails, to the fire of the fruit, and echoed again in the sunset behind Hymettus, and dropped in the cool aquamarine of the waves near the shore, and deepened into sapphire as I hung over the sides of the ship above the moving water. From this rich canvas I had come to the grays and greens and browns of England, the dove after the bird of Paradise, and, do you know, I felt the relationship of the two, the relationship of labour between the Greek, the almost pirate, crew, and the English farmer with his classic and primitive tools, the brotherhood between the sweeping scythe and the dipping oar, between the unwieldy stack and the clumsy vessel.

'The scent of the hay is in my nostrils, and the stirring is in my arms to throw up my fork-load upon the cart. We worked sometimes till ten at night, a race with the weather; we worked by sunlight and moonlight, and I preferred the latter. You may think that I preferred it because it pleased me to see the round yellow moon come up from behind the trees, and light that wholesome scene with its unwholesome radiance? Well, you are wrong, I am perhaps less perverse than you think me. I preferred it because I got less hot.

'Rawdon Westmacott used to come over to help us. A pair of extra hands was welcome, but I think old Pennistan would rather the hands had been tied on to any other body.

It was quite clear that he neglected his own farm only to be near Ruth, and I had long since gathered that the Pennistans would never willingly consider him as a son-in-law. I sympathised with them. He was an unruly man, as wild as he was handsome, a byword among the young men of the countryside; prompt with his fists – that was perhaps the best thing that could be said of him – foul with his tongue, intolerable when in his cups. So quarrelsome was he that even when sober he would seek out cause for insult. I myself, who in my capacity of guest, took every precaution to avoid any unpleasantness, had an ominous encounter with him. I had spent a day in London, and returned with various little gifts which I had thought would please the Pennistans; to Ruth I brought a pair of big, round, brass ear-rings and a coloured scarf, for I had a fancy to see her tricked out as a gipsy. It entertained me to see her, who as I told you was habitually slow of mind, enthusiasm, and speech, respond with some latent instinct to the gaudy things. She ran to the glass in the kitchen and began to screw the rings on to her unpierced ears.

' "You must learn to dance now, Ruth," I said.

'She looked round at me, and in the turn of her head and the flash of the rings I seemed to see Concha of the gipsy booth.

' "Father doesn't hold with dancing," she replied.

' "He isn't here to see," I said. "Won't you try a step?"

'She blushed. It was a pretty sight to see her blush.

' "I don't know how," she said awkwardly, looking away from me into the glass as she wound the scarf round her neck.

' "Well," I said, "will you learn if I have you taught?"

'She burst into the shrill laugh of the common girl, and cried, "Get along with you, Mr Malory! making fun of a poor girl like me."

'Concha was gone, but I struggled to revive her, without

55

conviction, and with a queer blankness in my heart. At least,' said Malory correcting himself, 'it wasn't my heart, but my mind, my sense of rightness, that was disappointed.

' "I mean it," I said. "I'll have you taught the dances of Spain."

' "Spain?" she echoed, with a frown genuinely puzzled, so remote from her was all thought of the land of her wandering forefathers.

'I risked a bold remark.

' "Your great-grandmother, I've no doubt, could give you a hint of the Spanish dances."

'Then she remembered, but the recollection came to her, I could see, from afar off, with the unreality of a date in history, poignant enough at the time.

'At that moment a knock fell upon the door, and Rawdon Westmacott came in without waiting to be bidden. He saw Ruth standing there, and stopped. Then he caught sight of me by the wide fireplace. His eyes travelled swiftly between us, and I saw the rage and the prompt conclusion spring into them. In fact, I never saw a man so suddenly full of barely contained anger. He would have given a great deal, I am sure, to have insulted me openly.

'We stood for a moment in silence, the three of us, then Westmacott's voice came out of space to break the moment's eternity.

' "That's fine toggery, Ruth, you've got on," he said.

'She looked at him without answering, her breath beginning to come a little quicker. I watched them both; I was angry, but not too angry to be interested. I felt the man's power; his brutality; and I remember thinking that something in her – was it primitive woman – responded to something – was it primitive man? – in him. At the same time I knew that waves of hatred vibrated between them; that, if she was attracted, she was no less repelled. Did I touch then, in an unexpected moment of insight, the vital spot of that enigma? I believe that I was very near the truth. I knew that the situation was not by any means an important one, but it was nevertheless a battle, a clash of wills, and as such I thought it significant.

'I saw her hand travel upward, and slowly begin to unwind the scarf.

'"It's ill becoming you, my girl," he went on, with the threatening note rising in his voice. "I'd sooner see you simple, Ruth," and I thought of the lashing sea when the wind begins to swirl like a dragon's tail along the beach.

'I tried to intervene.

'"I brought . . ." I began to say, but catching the glance which Ruth turned upon me I was silent.

'"You'd best take them off," Westmacott said.

'Slowly she took off the scarf, and laid it on the table, slowly she unfastened the rings and laid them beside the scarf. I could have wrung his neck, but for the sake of the girl I remained quiet; I knew that she would have to pay for my championship, and, besides, I was ignorant of what understanding existed between them. Underneath my anger, I was conscious of a vague irritation creeping over me, that she had taken his bullying so meekly and had not flown out at him, with her brass ear-rings clanking in her ears, as she had flown out at me on the day of Penshurst.

'Westmacott was clever enough to ignore the obvious fact that I had been the giver of the ornaments. He swept them off the table into his pocket, and, I presume, threw them into the horse-pond, and would have liked to throw me after; but that Ruth should not go without a present I ordered for her a pair of mice in a cage, a brown mouse and a Japanese waltzing mouse. She thought it extremely diverting to see the black and white mouse turning unceasingly after its tail, while the brown mouse watched it in perplexity mingled with disapproval from a corner of the cage.'

IV

'EITHER Westmacott did not notice these new inhabitants of the kitchen window-sill, for there they lived, among the pots of red geranium, or he considered he had humiliated me sufficiently; at any rate he made no allusions to the cage. As for Ruth and I, we went for several uncomfortable days without reference to the scene, but there it was between us, an awkward bond, until she broke the silence.

'We were in the dairy; I had brought in the newly-filled milk pails, and she stood churning butter upon a marble slab. I liked the dairy, with its great earthenware pans of milk, its tiled floor, and its cleanliness like the cleanliness of a ship. To-day it was full of the smell of the butter-milk.

' "Mr Malory," said Ruth suddenly turning to me. "I've never thanked you for understanding me the other night. I didn't think any the worse of you, I'd like to say, for keeping back your words."

' "So long as you didn't think I was afraid of your savage young friend . . ." I said.

' "No, no, I didn't think that," she answered with her quick blush. "He says more than he means, Rawdon does, if he's roused, and it's best to give in."

' "You give in a good deal to people," I said with that same irritation at her meekness.

' "It's easier . . ." she murmured.

'Ah? so that was it? not tameness of spirit, but mere indolence? I felt strangely comforted. At the same time I thought I would take advantage of our enforced confidences to make some remark about the young man of whom her parents had disapproved.

' "Westmacott . . ." I said. "He must be a difficult man

58

to deal with? Even for you, whose word should be law to him?"

'But my attempt wasn't a success, for she shut up like a box with a spring in the lid. I saw that I should never get her to discuss Rawdon Westmacott with me, and I came to the conclusion that she must be fond of the fellow, and I could understand it, regrettable as I thought it, for he was an attractive man in his dare-devil way.

'I soon had cause to regret my conclusion more, for I surprised the secret of a young handy-man who worked sometimes on the farm and for whom I had always had a great liking. He came to fell timber when old Pennistan wanted him, and he also did the thatching of the smaller, out-lying stacks. I went to help him at this work one day when his mate was laid up with a sprained ankle. He told me he had learnt his craft from his father, who had been a thatcher for fifty years; it gave me great satisfaction to think that a man could spend half a century on so mono-tonous a craft, constantly crawling on the sloping tops of ricks, with a bit of carpet tied round his knees, and his elementary tools – a mallet, a long wooden comb, a bundle of sticks, and a pocketful of pegs – always ready to his hand, while his mate on the ground pulled out the straw from the golden truss, made the ends even, and lifted the prepared bundle on a pitchfork up to the thatcher. My young friend told me the art of thatching was dying out. I tried my hand at it, but the straw blew about, and I found I could not lay two consecutive strands in place.

'He was a fine young man, whose knowledge of the country seemed as instinctive as it was extensive. I said I surprised his secret. I should not have used the word sur-prise. It shouted itself out from his candid eyes as he rested them on Ruth; she had brought out his dinner, and leaned against his ladder for a moment's talk; he looked down at her from where he knelt on the rick, and if ever I saw adoration in a man's face I saw it on his just then. I felt angry with Ruth in her serene unconsciousness. She had no right to disturb men with her more than beauty. I wondered whether she was or was not pledged to Rawdon Westmacott, and the more of a riddle she appeared to me the angrier I felt against her.

'I was dissatisfied with the whole situation; I could not manipulate my puppets as I would; I felt that I held a handful of scattered pearls, and could find no string on which to hang them. In my discontent I went into the kitchen to look at the mice, they were still and huddled in separate corners. Amos and his wife were sitting at the table drinking large cups of tea, Amos, full-bearded, and in his shirt sleeves and red braces as I had first seen him. As I turned to go they stopped me.

'"Mr Malory," Amos said, "we'd like to ask your advice. We're right moidered about our girl. We've seen how it is between her and young Westmacott. Now we'll not have young Westmacott in our family if we can help it, and we're wondering whether it would be best to forbid him the place, and forbid Ruth to hold any further truck with him, or to trust her good sense to send him about his business in the end."

'I reflected Then I considered that Wesmacott was probably more attractive present than absent, and spoke.

'"I hardly like to interfere in what isn't really my affair at all, but as you've asked me I'll say that if Ruth were my daughter I should forbid him the farm."

'"That clinches it," said Amos, bringing his hand down on the table. "We'll have the girl in and tell it her straight away. You've voiced my own feelings, sir, and I'm grateful to you."

'Here Mrs Pennistan began to cry.

'"My poor Ruth! and what if she's fond of the boy?"

' "Better for her to shed a dozen tears for him now than a hundred thousand in years to come. I'll call her in."

'She came, wiping her hands on her blue apron.

' "Father, the butter'll spoil."

' "Never mind the butter. Now listen here, my girl, we've been talking about you, your mother and I, and we've decided that you and Rawdon have seen more of each other than is good for you. So I'm going to tell him that he's to keep over at his own place in the future, and I expect you to keep over here; that is, I won't have you slipping out and meeting that young good-for-nothing when the fancy takes you."

'What a gentleman he is, I thought to myself, to have kept my name out of it.

'I looked at Ruth, wondering what she would do, and hoping, yes, hoping that she would rebel.

' "Very well, dad," was all she said, and she looked perfectly composed, and was not even twisting her apron as she stood there before the court of justice.

'I think Amos was a little surprised, a little disappointed, at her compliance.

' "You understand?" he said, trying to emphasise the point which he had already gained. "No skylarking."

' "I understand, dad," she said, still in that quiet and perfectly respectable voice.

' "There's a good girl," said Mrs Pennistan, and she got up and kissed her daughter, who submitted passively.

' "Now perhaps Mr Malory'll lend me a hand with the butter, or it'll spoil," said Ruth, looking at me, and I followed her out to the dairy, expecting, I must confess, that she would turn upon me and rend me. But she remained severely practical as she set me to my task.

'I could bear it no longer.

' "Ruth," I said, "I must be honest with you, even though

61

it makes you angry. Your father asked my advice in this business, and I gave it him."

' "You shouldn't stop," she said, "the butter'll never set properly."

'I returned to my churn.

' "But, Ruth, do you understand what I say? I am partly responsible for Westmacott's dismissal."

'Her hand and arm continued their rotary movement, but she turned her large eyes upon me.

' "Why?" she inquired, with disconcerting simplicity.

' "I don't like him," I muttered. "How could I live here, knowing you married to a man I dislike and mistrust?"

'To my surprise she said no more, but bent to her work, and I saw a great blush like a wave creep slowly over her half hidden face and down where her unfastened dress revealed her throat.

' "Ruth," I said humbly, "are you angry with me?"

'I heard a "No," that glided out with her breath.

' "I hope you don't care for him too much? He isn't worthy of you."

' "Can you lift that pail for me?" she said, pointing, and I lifted the heavy pail, and poured it as she directed into the separator, a smooth Niagara of milk.

'About three days later my thatcher unbosomed himself to me. Westmacott had disappeared from the farm, and of course every one for five miles round knew that Pennistan had turned him out. I don't know how they knew it, but country people seem to know things like a swallow knows its way to Egypt.

'I recommended my thatcher to speak privately to Amos first, which he did, and received that good man's sanction and approval.

'Then Ruth came to me, or, rather, I met her with the pig pail in her hand, and she stopped me. A distant reaper was singing on its way somewhere in the summer evening.

' "I've seen Leslie Dymock," she said abruptly. "Is it true that you . . ."

' "I didn't discourage him," I said as she paused.

'Again she put to me that disconcerting question, "Why?"

' "He's a good fellow," I answered warmly. "He cares for you. He didn't tell me. I guessed."

' "How?" she asked.

' "Heavens!" I cried, taking the pig pail angrily from her, "you positively rout me with your direct questions. Why? How? As if one's actions could hold in a single why or how. Don't you know that the stars of the Milky Way are as nothing compared with the complexity of men's motives?"

'She gazed at me, and as I looked into her eyes I felt that I had been a fool, and that with certain human beings a single motive could sail serenely like a rising planet in the evening sky. Then I remembered that I was still holding the pail. I set it down.

' "I am sorry," I said more gently, "I ought not to answer you like that. I like, I respect, and I trust Leslie Dymock, and for that reason I should at least be glad to see you consider his claim. As for my guessing, I had only to look at his face when you came."

' "I see," she said slowly. She bent to recover her pail. "I must be getting on to the pigs," and indeed those impatient animals were shrieking discordantly from the stye.

'Next day,' said Malory as though in parenthesis, and with a reminiscent smile on his face, 'I remember that a butcher came to buy the pigs. He fastened a big hook on to the beams of the ceiling in a little, dark, disused cottage, and we drove the pigs, three of them, into the cottage for the purpose of weighing them alive, and Ruth looked on from outside, through the much cobwebbed window. It was a scene both farcical and Flemish. All the farm dogs gathered round barking; the pigs, who were terrified into panic, made

63

an uproar such as you cannot imagine if you have never heard a pig screaming. The butcher and his mate drove them into sacks, head first, and as he got the snout neatly into one corner of the sack, and the feet into as many corners as were left to accommodate them, the sack took on the exact semblance of a pig dragging itself with restraint and difficulty along the ground. One after the other they were hoisted into the air and suspended yelling from the hook. I went out to see whether Ruth was scared by the noise. She was not. She was laughing as I had never seen her laugh before, her hands pressed to her hips, tears in her eyes, her white teeth gleaming in the shadows. I was interested, because I thought I understood the inevitable introduction of farcical interludes into mediæval drama. Now I think I understand better, that Ruth, who entirely lacked a sense of the humorous in life, was rich in the truly Latin sense of farce. I practised on her on several occasions after that, and never failed to draw the laugh I expected. The physical imposition of the automatic was unvarying in its results. And she had no feminine sentimentality about the sufferings of the pigs – not she. She rather liked to see animals baited.'

Yes, my friend, thought I as he paused, and I understand you even better than you profess to have understood the girl. You have no spark of real humour in your composition.

Just as Malory reached this point in his story, I was obliged to go away to Turin for a couple of days, but my mind ran more on the Weald of Kent than on my own affairs: I felt that the summer days were slipping by, that the corn would be cut and set up in stooks, if not already carted, by the time I got back, and that Leslie Dymock might have made such good use of his time as to be actually betrothed. As soon as I reached Sampiero and had changed from my travelling decency into my habitual flannels, I rushed out to find Malory, who was sitting with his pipe in his mouth beside the stream fishing.

He greeted me, 'I've caught two trout.'

'No? We'll have them for breakfast,' and I threw myself upon the ground beside him, and watched his lazy line rocking on the water.

'What it is to be a fisherman!' Malory said. 'To wade out into a great, broad river, and stand there isolated from men, with the water swirling round your knees, and crying "Come! come away from the staid and stupid land out to the sea, and exchange the shackles of life for the liberty of death." When the voice of the water has become too insistent, I have all but bent my knees and given myself up to the rhythm of the stream. Fishing, like nothing else, begets serenity of spirit. Serenity of spirit,' he repeated, 'and turbulence of action – that should make up the sum of man's life.'

He cast his fly and began to murmur some lines over to himself,—

> 'Give me a spirit that on life's rough sea
> Loves t' have his sails filled with a lusty wind,
> Even till his sail-yards tremble, his masts crack,
> And his rapt ship run on her side so low
> That she drinks water, and her keel ploughs air.
> There is no danger to a man that knows
> What life and death is. . . . .'

'The Elizabethans counted life well lost in an adventurous cause. I believe in their sense of duty, but I believe still more in their sense of adventure. And they share with the French the love of *panache*. Prudence is a hateful virtue. I believe the hatefulness of prudence is the chief cause of the unpopularity of Jews.'

He looked apologetically at me to see what I made of his dogmatic excursion.

'I wonder whether you want me to go on with my story? You do! Well. Amos Pennistan said to me after a month had passed, "I've enough of Ruth's nivvering-novvering."

'I thought that,' said Malory, 'an excellent expression – a moral onomatopœia. Amos continued, "I'm going to say to her, 'One thing or the other; either you take Leslie Dymock, or you leave him.' " "Grand!" I said, "I like your directness, straight to the point, like a pin to a magnet. After all, over-much subtlety has weakened modern life and modern art alike. And what if she replies that she will leave him?"

'I thought his answer a fine simple one, patriarchal in its pride: "There's many young men besides Leslie Dymock that would be glad to marry my daughter; 'tis not every girl has such a dower of looks as my girl, and a dower of this world's goods thrown along." Flocks and herds, she-goats and he-goats, I suppose he would have said, had he lived in Israel two thousand years ago.

'So this ultimatum was presented to Ruth, who asked for a month in which to make up her mind. I saw her going about her work as usual, but I supposed that thoughts more sacred, more speculative, than her ordinary thoughts of daily labour, were coming and going in her brain, hopping, and occasionally twittering, like little birds in a coppice. I did not speak to her much at this time. I pictured her as a nun during her novitiate, or as a young man in vigil beside his unused armour, or as the condemned criminal in his cell, because all three figures share alike a quality of aloofness from the world. I only wished that Heaven might grant me a second Daphnis and Chloe for my depopulated Arcady, and I asked no greater happiness than to see Ruth and Leslie tangled together in the meshes of love.

'September was merging into October, and again the orchards on the slope of the hill were loaded with fruit, the bushel baskets stood on the ground and the tall ladders

66

reared themselves into the branches. We were all fruit-pickers for the time being. Of the apples, only the very early kinds were ripe for market, and of this I was glad, for I enjoyed the jewelled orchard, red, green, and russet, and yellow, too, where the quince-trees stood with their roots under the little brook, but the plums were ready, and the village boys swarmed into the trees to pick such fruit as their hands could reach, and to shake the remainder to the ground. We, below, stood clear while a shower of plums bounced and tumbled into the grass, then we filled our baskets with gold and purple, returning homewards in the evening laden like the spies from the Promised Land. Amos stood, nobly apostolic, his great beard spread like a breast-plate over his chest, among the glowing plunder. I was re-minded of my Greek trader, and of the Tuscan vineyards; and the English country and the southern plenty were again strangely mingled.

'Towards the end of the month, considering that if her mind had not yet sailed into the sea of placidity I so desired it to attain, it would never do so, I decided to sound Ruth upon her decision. You see, she interested me, disappointed as I was in her, and I had nothing else to think about at the time save these, to you no doubt tame, love affairs of my country friends. I had a good deal of difficulty in coaxing her into a sufficiently emotional frame of mind; as fast as I threw the ballast out of our conversational balloon, she threw in the sand-bags from the other side. My speech was all of the lover's Heaven, hers of the farm-labourer's earth. She was curiously on the defensive; I could not understand her. I was certain that her matter-of-factness was, that evening, deliberate. She was full of restraint, and yet, a feverishness, an expectancy clung about her, which I could not then explain, but which I think was fully explained by later events.

'We got off at last, we went soaring up into the sky; it

was my doing, for I had uttered the wildest words to get her to follow me. I had talked of marriage; Heaven knows what I said. I told her that love was passion and friendship – passion in the secret night, but comradeship in the open places under the sun, and that whereas passion was the drunkenness of love, friendship was its food and clear water and warmth, and bodily health and vigour. I told her that children were to their begetters what flowers are to the gardener: little expanding things with dancing butterflies, sensitive, responsive, satisfying; the crown of life, the assurance of the future, the rhyme of the poem. I told her that in love alone can the poignancy of joy equal the poignancy of sorrow. I told her of that minority that finds its interest in continual change, and of that majority which rests on a deep content, and a great many other things which I do not believe, but which I should wish to believe, and which I should wish all women to believe. I told her all that I had never told a human being before, all that I had, perhaps, checked my tongue from uttering once or twice in my life, because I knew myself to be an inconstant man. I made love by quadruple proxy, not as myself to Ruth Pennistan, or as myself in Leslie Dymock's name to Ruth Pennistan, or as myself to any named or unnamed woman, but as any man to any woman, and I enjoyed it, because sincerity always carries with it a certain degree of pain, but pure rhetoric carries the pure enjoyment of the creative artist.'

I disliked Malory's cynicism, and I should have disliked it still more had I not suspected that he was not entirely speaking the truth. I was also conscious of boiling rage against the man for being such a fool.

'When I had finished,' he went on, 'she was trembling like a pool stirred by the wind.

' "You think like that," she said, "I never heard any one talk like that before."

'Then I told her a great deal more, about her Spanish

heritage and that disturbing blood in her veins, and about Spain, of which she knew next to nothing: that southern Spain was soft and the air full of orange-blossom, but that the north was fierce and arid, and peopled by men who in their dignity and reserve had more in common with the English than with the Latin races to whom they belonged; that as their country had not the kindliness of the English country, so they themselves lacked the kindly English humour, which mocks and smiles and, above all, pities; and that their temper is not swift, but slow like the English temper, but, when roused, ruthless and as little to be checked as a fall of water. I think that for the first time she guessed at a world beyond England, a world, that is, inhabited by real men. Before that, Spain and all Europe had been as remote as the stars.'

Malory told her all this, and then, when they were fairly flying through the air – I imagined them as the North Wind and the little girl in the fairy-story: hair streaming, garments streaming, hand pulling hand – he judged the moment opportune to return to Leslie Dymock. I fancy that the crash to earth again must have knocked all consciousness from the girl for a considerable interval. During this interval Malory dilated on the admirableness of the young man, his estimable qualities, and his worldly prospects. I could understand his scheme. He had planned to fill her with electricity, then to switch her suddenly off, sparkling and thrilling, on to Leslie Dymock. He had, I suppose, assumed that a certain sympathy had already inclined her native tenderness towards Leslie Dymock. The scheme was an excellent one in all but one particular: that his initial premise was radically false.

After the interval of her unconsciousness, she returned with slowly opening eyes to what he was saying. God knows what she had expected the outcome of their wild journey to be. Malory only told me that with parted lips and eyes in

69

which all the mysteries of awakened adolescence were stirring, she laid her hand, a trembling hand, on his hand and
said,—

'What do you mean? why do you speak to me like . . .
like this, and then talk to me again about Leslie Dymock?'

He asked her whether she could not find her happiness
with Leslie Dymock and realise in her life with him all the
pictures whose colours he, Malory, had painted for her. And
she answered so bitterly and so scornfully that he charged
her with having her heart still fixed on Rawdon Westmacott.

'Still fixed!' she cried, emphasising the first word, 'and
how could that be still fixed which never was fixed at all?'

He was baffled; he thought her an unnatural creature to be
still heart-whole when her youth, her advantages, and that
depth which, in spite of her tameness, her reserve, and his
own protestations of her lack of passion – protestations
which I suspect he continued to make for the strengthening
of his own unsure belief – he instinctively divined, should
have created a tumult in her soul. It was to him unthinkable
that such hammer-strokes as Nature, Westmacott, and
Dymock had conjointly delivered on the walls of her heart,
should have failed to open a breach. Such breaches, once
opened, are hard to close against a determined invader. He
urged her to confide in him, he told her that his whole delight lay in the problems of humanity, that metaphysics and
psychology were to his mind as sea-air to his nostrils. She
only looked at him, and I think it was probably fortunate
for his vanity that he could not read what a fool she thought
him. I suppose that every man must appear to a woman half
a genius and half a fool. Much as a grown person must appear to the infinitely simpler and infinitely more complex
mind of a child.

He urged her confidence, therefore, seeing that she remained silent, although her lips were still parted, her hand

still lying on his hand, and the expectation still living in her eyes, that had not as yet remembered to follow the lead of her mind. They were the mirrors of her instinct, and her instinct was at variance with her reason. He had come down to the practical business of his mission, while she lived still in the enchanted moments of their flight into a realm to her unknown. If her ears received his emphatic words, her brain remained insensible to them. He detached his hand from hers, to lay it on her shoulder and to shake her slightly.

'Ruth! do you hear what I am saying to you?'

Her widened eyes contracted for an instant, as with pain, and turning them on him she prepared an expression of intelligent comprehension to greet his next sentence.

'I am asking you to trust me as a friend. It's lonely to be left alone with a decision. If you are angry with me for interfering, tell me to go away, and I will go. But so long as I may talk to you, I want to keep my finger on the pulse of your affairs, where it has been, let me remind you, ever since I set foot in your father's house. I want to see you happy in your home, and to know that I accompanied you at any rate to the threshold.'

She broke from him, he told me, with a cry; ran from him, and never reappeared that evening. On the following day she accepted Leslie Dymock.

V

'THERE was a great deal of rejoicing,' Malory continued, 'in the Pennistan household over the engagement. Nancy and her husband came for a three days' visit. I was glad to see my Daphnis and Chloe's again, and to discover that all the sweets of marriage which I had described to Ruth were living realities in these two. They seemed insatiable for each other's presence. Their attitude towards Ruth and Leslie was parental; nay, grandfatherly; nay, ancestral! Experience and patronage transpired through the cracks of their benison. Ruth was annoyed, but I was greatly amused.

'It had been arranged that the wedding should take place almost immediately. Why delay? I am sure that Leslie Dymock was hungering to get his wife away to his own home. And Ruth? She accepted every happening with calm, avoided me – I suppose that she was shy, and left her to herself – was gentle and affectionate to Leslie, took a suitable interest in the preparations of her wedding. I was, on the whole, satisfied. I did not believe that she was much in love with Leslie Dymock, in fact I was inclined to think that she regretted her handsome blackguard, but I believed that her evident fondness for Dymock would develop with their intimacy, and that the bud would presently break out into the full-blown rose.

'As for him, he would not have exchanged his present position with an archangel.

'I asked Amos what had become of Westmacott.

' "Over at his place, like a wild beast in a cave," he replied with a grin.

' "Is he coming to the wedding?"

' "Oh, ay, if he chooses."

72

'I now became concerned for my own future. Life at the Pennistans' without Ruth would, I foresaw, be less agreeable although not actually unbearable. She and I had worked together in a harmony I could scarcely hope to reproduce with the hired girl who was to take her place, for you must realise that although I have only reported to you our conversations on the more human subjects of life, our everyday existence had been made up of hours of happy work and mutual interest. I seriously thought of leaving, and said as much to Dymock.

'Some days afterwards that good young man came to me.

'"I've been thinking," he said, "of your leaving and of your not liking, as you told me, to go away from the Weald till after next spring. Now I've a proposal to make to you," and he told me of a cottage near his own place, with five acres, enough to support hens, pigs, and a cow, whose tenant had recently died. He suggested to me that I should rent this small holding for a year. "And you can walk over o' nights, and have a bit of supper with us," he added hospitably.

'The matter was adjusted, and I told Ruth with joy that I should be within half a mile of her in her new life. I was grieved to see that she first looked taken aback, then dismayed, then irritated. I say that I was grieved, but presently I found occasion to be glad, for I reflected that if she thus resented the disturbance of her solitude with her husband it could only be on account of her growing fondness for him, and as I could not now revoke my tenancy I resolved that I would at least be a discreet neighbour.

'How smugly satisfied we all were at that time! I feel ashamed for myself and for the others when I think of it.

'The first indication I had that anything was wrong came about a week before Ruth's wedding, when, walking down a lane near Pennistans', driving home the cattle, I passed Rawdon Westmacott. We were by then near November, so

73

the evening was dark, and I was not sure of the man's identity until we had actually crossed. Then I saw his sharp face, and recognised the subtly Oriental lilt of his walk. He looked angry when he saw that I was myself, and not one of the herdsmen he no doubt expected. I wondered what the fellow was doing on Pennistan's land.

'The weather was bitterly cold, all the leaves were gone from the trees, and the fat, wealthy Weald was turned to a scarecrow presentment of itself. Instead of the blue sky and great white prancing clouds like the Lord Mayor's horses, a hard sulphur sky greeted me in the early mornings, with streaks of iron gray cloud on the horizon, and a lowering red disc of sun. Underfoot the ground was frosty, and the frozen mud stood up in little sharp ridges. As it thawed during the day the clay resumed its slimy dominion, and I had to exchange my shoes for boots, as the clay pulled my shoes off my heels.

'It was now two days before the wedding, and I sought out Ruth to make her my humble present. Never mind what it was. I had got her an extra present, which, I told her, was my real offering, and I gave her the case, and she opened it on a pair of big brass ear-rings. She got very white.

' "You can wear them now," I said, "Leslie at least isn't jealous of me, and here is the rest," and I gave her the coloured scarf.

'She took it from my hand, never thanking me or saying a word, but looking at me steadily, and put the scarf round her throat.

'I added my good wishes; Heaven knows they were sincere.

' "Tell me you're happy, Ruth, and I shall be filled with gladness."

' "I'm happy," she said dully.

' "And you're fond of Leslie?"

' "Yes," she said with such sudden emphasis that I was

74

startled, "all that you said about him is true; he is kind and valiant, a man with whom any woman should be happy. I am glad that I have learnt how good he is. I am fonder of him than of my brothers."

'I thought that a strange comparison, but not wholly a bad one.

'I tried to be hearty.

'"I am so pleased, Ruth, and my vanity is gratified, too, for I almost think you might have passed him by but for me."

'"Yes," she said, "yes, I would have passed him by."

'"By God, Ruth!" I burst out, "he is a lucky fellow. Do you know that you are a very beautiful woman?"

'She swayed as though she were dizzy for a moment.

'"I must go," she said then, "and I haven't said thank you, but I do thank you."

'She paused.

'"You have taught me a great deal. I have learnt from you what men like Leslie Dymock have a right to expect from life."

'"And you will give it him?" I asked.

'She bowed her head.

'"I will try."

'Now I thought that a very satisfactory conversation, and I went about my work, for beasts must be fed and housed, weddings or no weddings, with a singing heart that day. If, somewhere, a tiny worm of jealousy crawled about on the floor-mud of my being, I think I bottled it very successfully into a corner. I was not jealous of Dymock on account of Ruth; no, not exactly; but jealous only as one must be jealous of two young happy things when one remembers that, much as one values one's independence, one is not the vital life-spark of any other human being on this earth. There must be moments when the most liberty-loving among us envy the yoke they fly from.

'I clapped a cow on her ungainly shallow flanks as I tossed up her bedding, and said to her, "You and I, old friend, must stick together, for if man can't have his fellow-creatures to love he must return to the beasts." She turned her glaucous eye on me as she munched her supper. Then I heard voices in the shed.

'"Rawdon! if dad sees you . . ."

'And Westmacott's hoarse voice.

'"I'll chance that, but, by hell, Ruth, you shall listen to me. They think you're going to marry that lout, but as I'm a living man you shan't. I'll murder him first. I swear before God that if you become that man's wife I'll make you his widow."

'I stood petrified, wondering what I should do. It was night, and pitch dark inside the shed, but as I looked over the back of my cow down the line of stalls in which the slow cattle were lazily ruminating, I saw two indistinct figures and, beyond them, the open door, the night sky, and an angry moon, the yellow Hunters moon, rising behind the trees.

'Ruth spoke again.

'"Rawdon, don't talk too loud. I'll stay, yes, I'll stay with you; only dad'll kill you if he finds you here."

'"I've been up every night to find you," Westmacott said in a lower voice. "I've hung about hoping you'd come out. Ruth, you don't know. I'm mad for you. . . . You're my woman. What business have you to go with bloodless men? You come with me, and I'll give you all you lack. I'll be good to you, too, I swear I will. I'll not drink; no, on my word, it's the thought of you that drives me to it. Ruth!"

'He put out his arms and tried to seize her, but she recoiled and stood holding on to the butt-end of a stall.

'"Hands off me, Rawdon."

'"You're very particular," he sneered; and then, changing his tone, "Come, child, you're just ridiculous. I know you better than that. Have you forgotten the day we drove to Tonbridge market? you wasn't so nice then."

'"I disremember," she said stolidly, but under her stolidity I think she was shaken.

'"You don't disremember at all. There's fire in you, Ruth, there's blood; that's why I like you. You're shamming ladylike. I've got that gent with his accursed notions to thank, I suppose."

'This reminded me with a start of my own identity. I could not stay eavesdropping, so I made up my mind and stepped out into the passage between the stalls.

'Westmacott and Ruth cried simultaneously,—

'"Who's that?"

'"Mr Malory!"

'"This is a bad hour for you, sir," said Westmacott to me.

'I knew that I must not quarrel with him.

'"I am sorry," I said. "I had no intention of spying on you and was only doing my ordinary work in here. I will go if you, Ruth, wish me to go."

'"No," said Westmacott, "go, and tell them all I'm here? Not much. You've heard enough now to know I want Ruth. You've always known it. I've always wanted her, and I mean to have her. Who are you, you fine gentleman, that you should stand in my way? I could crush your windpipe with my finger and thumb."

I pictured that grotesque scene in that dark, smelly shed, among the ruminating cattle, and those two antagonistic men with the girl between them.

'I turned to Ruth,' said Malory, 'and asked her frigidly what she wanted me to do? Should I attack the fellow? or give the alarm? or was it by her consent that he was there? Again she did not speak and he answered for her.

'"I'm here by her consent, she's had a note from me,

77

and she answered it, and here she is. Isn't it true?" he demanded of her.

' "It is quite true," she said, speaking to me.

'I was hurt and disappointed.

' "Then I will go, as it appears to be an assignation."

' "No," said Ruth, "wait. You said you had had your finger on the pulse of my affairs ever since you came here, and now you must follow them out to the end. I am not a bit afraid of your turning me away from the path I've chosen."

'Weak! I had thought her. As I stood there like a bereft and helpless puppet between those two dark figures, I felt myself a stranger and a foreigner to them, baffled by the remoteness of their race. They were of the same blood, and I and Leslie Dymock were of a different breed, tame, contented, orderly, incapable of abrupt resolution. Weak! I had thought her. Well, and so she had been, indolently weak, but now, like many weak natures, strong under the influence of a nature stronger than her own. So, at least, I read her new determination, for I did not believe in a well of strength sprung suddenly in the native soil of her being. I perceived, rather, a spring gushing up in the man, and pouring its torrent irresistibly over her pleasant valleys. I thought her the mouthpiece of his thunder. At the same time, something in her must have risen to merge and marry with the force of his resolve. Who knows what southern blood, what ancient blood, what tribal blood, had stirred in her from slumber? what cry of the unknown, unseen wild had drawn her towards a mate of her own calibre? An absurd joy rushed up in me at the thought. I flung a dart of sympathy to Leslie Dymock, but he, like those slow-chewing cattle, was of the patient, long-suffering sort whose fate is always to be cast aside and sacrificed to the egoism of others. I forgot my homily on marriage, and the pictures I had drawn of Ruth and Dymock in their happy home with their quiverful of robust and flaxen children. I forgot the sinful lusts of Rawdon Westmacott. Yes, I lost myself wholly in the joy of the mating of two Bohemian creatures, and in Ruth's final justification of herself.

' "I want you," continued Ruth, in the same even, relentless voice, "to stand by Leslie whatever may come to him, and to show him that he's a happier man for losing me . . ."

'I heard Westmacott in the darkness give a snarl of triumph.

' "You're determined, then?" I said to Ruth. "You've not had much time to make up your mind, or wasted many words over it, since I surprised you here."

' "Time?" she said, "words? A kettle's a long time on the fire before it boils over. I know I'm not for Leslie Dymock, I know it this evening, and I've known it a long while though I wouldn't own it. I'm going, and I want to be forgotten by all at home."

'I was moved by her homely little simile, and by the anguish in her voice at her last sentence.

' "I don't dissuade you," I said. "Dymock must recover, and if you and your cousin love one another . . ."

'Westmacott broke in bitterly,—

' "Say! You seem to have missed the point . . ."

' "Rawdon!" Ruth spoke with a passion I, even I, had not foreseen. "Rawdon, I forbid you to say another word."

'He grumbled to himself, and was silent.

'I looked at her during the pause in which she waited threateningly for signs of rebellion on his part, and I found in her face, lit by the light of the Hunter's moon, the strangest conflict that ever I saw on a woman's face before. I read there distress, soul-shattering and terrible, but I also read a determination which I knew no argument could weaken. She was unaware of my scrutiny, for her eyes were bent on Westmacott. Her glance was imperious; she knew herself to be the coveted woman for whose possession he must fawn and cringe; she knew that to-night she could command, if for ever after she would have to obey. I read this knowledge, and I read her distress, but above all I read recklessness, a wild defiance, which alarmed me.

' "I've said what I want to say," she added. "You've thought me a meek woman, Mr Malory, you've told me so, and so I am, but I seem to have come to a fence across my meekness, and I know neither you nor any soul on earth could hold me back. It's never come to me before like this. Maybe it'll never come again. Maybe you've helped me to it. There's much I don't know, much I can't say . . ." her ignorant spirit struggled vainly for speech. I was silent, for I knew that elemental forces were loose like monstrous bats in the shed which contained us.

' "Am I to say good-bye?" I asked.

'She swayed over towards me, as though the strength of her body were infinitely inferior to the strength of her will. She put her hands on my shoulders and turned me, so that the light of the yellow moon fell on my face.

'She said then,—

' "Kiss me once before I go."

'Rawdon started forward.

' "No, damn him!"

'She laughed.

' "Don't be a fool, Rawdon, you'll have me all your life."

'I kissed her like a brother.

' "Bless you, my dear, may you be happy. I don't know if you're wise, but I dare say this is inevitable, and things are not very real to-night."

'There was indeed something absurdly theatrical about the shed full of uneasily shifting cattle, and that great saffron moon – shining, too, on the empty arena of Cadiz.

'I left them standing in the shed, and got into the house by the back door; with methodical precision I replaced the key under the mat where, country-like, it always lived.'

I felt in my own mind that much remained which had not been satisfactorily explained, but when Malory resumed after a moment's pause, it was to say,—

'I don't know that there is very much more to tell. I came down at my usual hour the next morning, and found no signs of commotion about the farm. As a matter of fact, I caught sight of nobody but a stray labourer or so as I went my rounds. I moved in a dull coma, such as overtakes us after a crisis of great excitement; a dull reaction, such as follows on some deep stirring of our emotions. Then as I went in to breakfast, I saw Mrs Pennistan moving in the kitchen in her habitual placid fashion, and Amos came in, rubbing his hands on a coarse towel, strong and hearty in the crisp morning. The old grandmother was already in her place by the fire, her quavering hands busy with her toast and her cup of coffee. Everything wore the look I had seen on it a hundred times before, and I wondered whether my experience had not all been a dream of my sleep, and whether Ruth would not presently arrive with that flush I had learnt to look for on her cheeks.

' "Where's Ruth?" said Mrs Pennistan as we sat down.

' "She'll be in presently, likely," said Amos, who was an easy-going man.

'Her mother grumbled.

' "She shouldn't be late for breakfast."

' "Come, come, mother," said Amos, "don't be hard on the girl on her wedding-eve," and as he winked at me I hid my face in my vast cup.

'Then Leslie Dymock burst in, with a letter in his hand, and at the sight of his face, and of that suddenly ominous little piece of white paper, the Pennistans started up and tragedy rushed like a hurricane into the pleasant room.

'He said,—

' "She's gone, read her letter," and thrust it into her father's hand.

'I wish I could reproduce for you the effect of that letter which Amos read aloud; it was quite short, and said, "Leslie. I am going away because I can't do you the injustice of becoming your wife. Tell father and mother that I am doing this because I think it is right. I am not trying to write more because it is all so difficult, and there is a great deal more than they will ever know, and I don't think I understand everything myself. Try to forgive me. I am, your miserable Ruth."

'I cannot tell you,' said Malory, who, as I could see, was profoundly shaken by the vividness of his recollection, 'how moved I was by the confusion and distress of those strangely disquieting words. I could not reconcile them at all with the picture I had formed of two kindred natures rushing at last together in a pre-ordained and elemental union. I rose to get away from the family hubbub, for I wanted to be by myself, but on the way I stopped and looked at the mice in their cage among the red geraniums. They were waltzing frantically, as though impelled by a sinister influence from which there was no escape.'

PART II

I

I CONTINUED to feel, as I have said, that there was much in Malory's story which remained to be satisfactorily explained, for I was convinced in my own mind that his interpretation of Ruth Pennistan's flight, plausible as it was, was totally misleading, with the dangerous verisimilitude of a theory which will fit all, or nearly all, the facts, and yet more entirely miss the truth, by a mere accident, than would a frank perplexity. I think that he himself secretly agreed with me, a conviction I arrived at less by his own doubting words after the reading of the letter, than by his manner towards me when he had finished the story, and his mute, but none the less absolute, refusal to discuss, as I in my interest would willingly have discussed, certain points in his narration. I received the impression that he had chosen me as his audience merely because we knew nothing of one another beyond our names, from a craving to pour out that long dammed-up flood of emotion and meditation. I had – a somewhat galling reflection – played the part of the ground to Malory's King Midas. I think that his indifference towards me turned to positive dislike after our week of intimacy, and this belief was strengthened when, with scarcely a farewell, he took an abrupt departure.

I will confess that I was hurt at the time, but an unaccountable instinct buoyed me up that some day, it might be after the passage of years, I should again be thrown in contact either with him or with his *dramatis personæ*. How this came about I will now tell, though I do not pretend that any more mysterious purpose than my own desire intervened in the accomplishment of my hopes. Perhaps Malory would say that War was my fate, my god in the machine; perhaps it was; I do not know. The definition of fate is a vicious circle; like a little animal, say a mouse, turning after its tail.

I left Sampiero in 1914, a year after I had parted there from Malory, and my earlier prophecy justified itself, that our acquaintance would not be continued in our own country. In fact, amid the excitement of the war, I had almost forgotten the man, his habitual reticence, his sudden outburst into narrative, and the unknown, unseen people with whom that narrative had been concerned. But now as I idled disconsolately in London, discharged from hospital but indefinitely unfit for service, there stirred in my memory a recollection of the Pennistans, who were to me so strangely familiar, and I resolved that I would go for myself to pick up the thread where Malory had dropped it, to work on the fields where he had worked, and to probe into the lives he had tried to probe.

Hearing that the small help I could give would be welcome, I started out, much, I suppose, as Malory had started, with my bag in my hand, and reached the tiny station one evening in early April. The station-master directed me across the fields, by a way which I felt I already knew, and as I walked I wondered what had become of Malory; presumably he had turned his hand to a fighting trade, or had he sought some bizarre occupation congenial to him, in the bazaars of Bagdad, or in a North Sea drifter, or had the air called to him? I could not decide; perhaps the Pennistans would have news of his whereabouts.

But they had none. He had sent them a field post card from Gallipoli, and since then he had again disappeared; they did not seem very much surprised, and I guessed that in their slow instinctive way they had felt him to be a transitory, elusive man, who might be expected to turn up in his own time from some unanticipated corner. They suggested, however, that I should walk over to Westmacotts' on a Sunday, and inquire from their daughter Ruth about Mr Malory.

I cannot say that I was unhappy at the Pennistans, for, though I fretted a good deal at my comparative inactivity, the peace and stability of the place, of which Malory had so often spoken, stole over me with gradual enchantment of my spirit, like the incoming tide steals gradually over the sands. During the first days I took a curious delight in discovering the spots that had figured in his story, the fields, the dairy, and the cow-shed, in recognising the pungent farm smells which had pleased his alert senses. These things were the same, but in other respects much was changed. The three bullock-like sons were gone, and few men remained to work the land. Rawdon Westmacott, they told me, was at the war, so was Nancy's husband. And on sunny days I used to watch the aeroplanes come sailing up out of the blue, the sun catching their wings, and tumble, for sheer joy it seemed, in the air, while the hum of their engines filled the whole sky as with a gigantic beehive.

One detail I noticed after several days. The cage of mice which Malory had given to Ruth was no longer in the place I expected to see it, on the kitchen window-sill.

The unexpected had favoured me in one particular. Malory had mentioned that the old woman was ninety-six in the year he had gone to Pennistans', and although he had never, so far as I remembered, given a date to that year, I reckoned that she must, if alive now, have passed her century. I was certain I should find her gone. Yet the first thing I saw as I entered the house was that little old huddled figure by the fire, head nodding, hands trembling, alive enough to feed and breathe, but not alive enough for anything else; she spent all her days in a wheeled chair, sometimes in the kitchen, sometimes in her own room, the quondam parlour, on the ground-floor across the passage; sometimes, when it was very warm, beside the garden-door out in the sun. She must always have been tiny, but now the frailty of her shrunken form was pitiable. Her wrists were like the legs of a chicken. Her jaws were fallen in, thin and flabby; her eyes never seemed to blink, but stared straight in front of her, at nothing, through everything. . . .

I had Malory's bedroom. It was bare, white-washed, monastic, and appeared to me peculiarly suitable as a shrine to his personality. I wondered whether he had spent any part of his wandering life in the seclusion of a cloister, and as I wondered the realisation came over me that Malory was in spirit nearly allied to those mediæval scholars, so unassuming, so far removed from the desire of fame, as to dedicate their anonymous lives to a single script, finding in their own inward satisfaction the fulfilment of personal ambition. And as I thought on Malory, in that clean, bare room, I came to a closer understanding of his kinship with many conditions of men, of his sympathy with life, nature, and craft – Malory, the man who had not been my friend.

As the week passed, I found myself greatly moved by the prospect of seeing, of speaking with Ruth. As I drew near to Westmacotts', I felt the physical tingling of intense excitement run over me. I was about to meet a dear companion, to hear the sound of her voice, and to look into the familiarity of her eyes. Another picture swam up out of the mist to dim my vision, a babbling music filled my ears like the sound of waves in a shell, and the faintest scent quivered under my nostrils; gradually as these ghosts emerged from the confusion I defined the Italian hill-side, the rushing stream, and the dry, aromatic scent of the ground. Was this, then, the setting in which Ruth walked and spoke for me? I was startled at the vividness of the impression, and at the incredibly subtle complexity of the ordinary brain.

Although Malory had never, so far as I could remember, given me any description of Westmacott's farm, whether of impression or detail, I recognised the place as soon as I had emerged from a little wood and had seen it lying in a hollow across the ploughed field, a connecting road which was little more than a cart-track running from it at right angles into the neat lane beyond. I recognised the farm-house, of creamy plaster heavily striped by gray oak beams, its upper storey slightly overhanging and supported on rounded corbels of the same bleached oak, rough-hewn. I was prepared to see, as I actually saw, the large barn of black, tarred weather-boarding, terminated by the two rounded oast-houses, and should have missed it had I not found it there.

And I knocked, and the sense of reality still failed to return to me. Someone opened the door. I saw a young woman in a blue linen dress, with a child in her arms, and other children clinging about her skirts. My first impression was of astonishment at her beauty; Malory had led me to expect a subtle and languorous seduction, but I was not prepared for such actual beauty as I now found in her face.

'Are you Mrs Westmacott?' I asked.

'Yes, sir,' she said, 'are you the gentleman that's stopping with father?'

'I see you know about me.'

'Yes, sir; mother was over yesterday, and said you'd likely be coming. Won't you come in, sir? if you'll excuse the children. There's only me to look after them to-day.'

I went into a clean and commonplace kitchen, and Ruth wiped a chair for me with her skirt, and put the baby into its cradle. She then sat down beside it, and with her foot kept the cradle moving on its rockers. I glanced round, and on the window-sill, among the pots of red geranium, I espied a wire cage with some little mice huddled in a corner.

'Mrs Westmacott,' I said, feeling that the beginning of the conversation rested with me, 'you and I are quite old

87

friends though you may not know it.' I hated myself for my jocularity. 'You remember Mr Malory? He has spoken to me about his life here, and about you.'

I was looking at her; I saw that marvellous, that red rose blush of which Malory had spoken, come up under her skin till her cheek was like the rounded beauty of a nectarine. And I wondered, as I had wondered before; I wondered ...

'And what news have you of Mr Malory?' she asked.

'None,' I said. 'I thought perhaps you might have heard.'

'I? If Mr Malory was to write at all, would he not have written to you? Why should he write to me?'

'I hope,' I said, 'that nothing has happened to him.'

She had answered me before I had finished speaking.

'Nothing has happened to him.'

'Why,' I said surprised, 'how are you so certain?'

She looked suddenly trapped and angry.

'It's an odd name,' she said at last, 'one would notice it in a casualty list.' She rushed on. 'We poor women, you know, have to keep our eye on the lists; there's few officers, but many men, a mistake's soon made, and my husband is there in France. This is my husband.' She lifted a photograph and showed me the keen, Arab face I had expected.

'Mr Malory always told me your husband was a very handsome man. Are any of your children like him?'

I wished that Malory could have seen the softening of her face when I spoke of her children.

'No, sir,' she said, and I could have sworn I heard an exultant note in her voice. 'They mostly take after their grandmother, I think,' and indeed I could see in the sleeping baby an absurd resemblance to Mrs Pennistan. 'Now my sister's children, she has two, and one is fair like her, and one is as dark as my husband.'

I do not know what impulse moved me to rise and go over to the cage of mice.

'I have heard of these, too, from Mr Malory,' I said. 'You have had them six, seven, eight years now?'

'Oh, sir,' she cried amused, 'those are not the pair Mr Malory gave me. Those are their great-great-great-great, I don't know how many greats, grandchildren. I've bred from them and bred from them; they're friendly little things, and the children like them.'

'How do they breed now?' I asked.

'Well,' she replied, 'they mostly come brown, I notice; I fancy the strain's wearing out. From time to time I'll get a black and white that doesn't waltz – waltzing mice Mr Malory used to call them – and from time to time I'll get a waltzer; there was a lot of them at first, one or two in a litter, but they're getting rare. That little fellow,' she said, pointing – and as she stood beside me I was conscious of her softness and warmth, and felt myself faintly troubled – 'I've known him waltz once only since I've had him, which is since he was born. I look at them,' she added unexpectedly, 'when they're blind and pink in the nest, and wonder which'll grow up brown and which'll waltz and which be just piebald.'

'You speak like Mr Malory,' I said.

She laughed as she turned away.

'Is that so, sir? Well, Mr Malory always liked the mice, I don't know why. He lived with us over a year, and maybe one takes on a manner of thinking in a year, I don't know.'

Somehow I felt that the section of our conversation dealing with Malory was closed by that remark. We hung fire for a little. Then I asked her to show me over the place, which she did, and after that we had tea in the kitchen, brown bread cut from the big loaf, honey from her own hives, and jam of her own making. I watched her as she laid the cloth, noted her quick efficiency, was conscious of her quiet reserve and her strength, saw her beauty foiled and trebled by the presence of her children. After tea she made me smoke a pipe, sent the children out to play, and sat opposite me in a rocking chair with sewing in her hands and more sewing heaped near her on the floor. It was very pleasant in that warm interior, the fire crackled, the big clock ticked. I thought what a fool Malory had been.

I walked home in the dusk, hearing what he had never heard from those meadows: the thudding and bruising of the distant guns.

II

LITTLE by little I learnt the details which linked the end of
Malory's story to the point where I was to take it up. Rawdon Westmacott, in spite of his wife's entreaties to settle in
another part of the country, had insisted on returning almost
directly after their marriage to his farm, and there, ignored
by her own family and by the whole horrified, scandalised
countryside, Ruth had dwelt in a companionship more terrible than solitude. For Westmacott had followed unbridled
his habitual paths of drunkenness and violence. How grim
and disquieting must have been that situation: not two
miles separated Pennistans' from Westmacotts', not two
miles lay between the parents and the daughter, yet they
were divided by league upon league of pride, across which
their mutual longing quivered as heat-waves upon the surface of the desert. The mother, I think, would have gone,
but Amos, with that Biblical austerity which Malory had
noted in him, forbade any advance towards, any mention
of, the prodigal. The ideal of decency, which is the main
ideal of the country people, had been outraged, and this
Amos, the heir of tradition, could not forgive. During the
greater part of the first year, neither Ruth nor her mother
can willingly have stirred far from their own garden door.
The torment, the gnawing of that self-consciousness! The
apprehension of that first Sunday, when Amos with set jaw
forced his wife to church! with what tremulousness she
must have entered the little nave, casting round her eyes in
secret, dreading yet hoping, relieved yet disappointed. She
bore traces of the strain, the buxom woman, in the covert
glance of her eyes and the listening, searching expression of
her face. I have seen her start at the sound of the door-latch,

and look up expectantly as she must have looked in those days, afraid and longing to see the beloved figure in the door.

The tension came to an end at last, for Nancy, whose will might not be crossed, burst out with indignation at the treatment of her sister and set off angrily for Westmacotts. She returned within an hour with the information that Rawdon was dead drunk in the kitchen and that Ruth's child would surely be born before morning. Mrs Pennistan had not known of the child; she leapt to her feet saying that she must go at once, and upbraided Amos for having withheld her so long from her own flesh and blood. Amos rose, and saying gloomily, 'Do what you will, but don't let me know of it,' he left the room.

I know nothing of the meeting between mother and daughter, but I imagine that the sheer urgency of the situation mercifully did much to smooth the difficulty of the moment. The crisis over, a new order of things replaced the old: relations were re-established, and Ruth henceforward came and went between her present and her former home. Only, the Pennistans' door was barred to the son-in-law, as their lips were barred to his name. At the most, his phantasm hovered between them.

Now I have told all that I could reconstruct, and most of this I heard from Nancy, who was a frank, outspoken girl; common, I thought her, and ordinary, but good-hearted underneath her exuberance. She had lived at home since her husband had gone to fight. She was very different from her quiet sister, as different as a babbling brook from a wide, calm pool of water. I heard a great deal of abuse of Westmacott from her, even to tales of how he ill-treated his wife; and I also heard of her own happiness, confidences unrestrainedly poured out, for she was innocent of reserve. To this I preferred to listen, though, truthfully, she often bored and sometimes embarrassed me. I soon discovered that for all her fiery temper she was a woman of no moral stamina, and I didn't like to dwell in my own mind upon her utter annihilation under the too probable blow of war.

The blow fell, and by the curse of Heaven I was there to see it; the reality of the danger had always seemed remote, even in the midst of its nearness, for such nightmares crawl closer and closer only to be flung back repeatedly by the force of human optimism. I had never before realised the depths of such optimism. Her first cry was 'It cannot be true!' her first instinct the instinct of disbelief. In the same way she had always clung to an encouraging word, however futile, and had been cast down to an equal degree by an expression of pessimism. I suppose that when the strings of the human mind are drawn so taut, the slightest touch will call forth their pathetic music. . . . Poor Nancy! I had seen her husband on leave for ten days during which her eyes were radiant and her voice busy with song; he went; and was killed the day after his return to France.

Not very long afterwards I got a letter from Malory, forwarded and re-forwarded, which, coming out of the, so far as he was concerned, silence of years, reminded me forcibly of the day he had broken silence at Sampiero. It gave me a queer turn of the heart to see that the envelope I held in my hand had gone first of all to Sampiero, to our little lodging house, had been handled, no doubt, by the hunch-backed postman I had known so well. I could see him, going down the street, with his bag over his shoulder, and my letter in his bag. I could see my old landlady with the letter in her hand, turning it over and over, till light broke on her, and she remembered the Englishman, and hunted up his unfamiliar address, and wondered, perhaps, whether he, too, had fallen in the war.

I give Malory's letter here.

'. . . I read his name in the official list, and can only suppose that it is my Daphnis, as I know he was in a Kentish regiment. Oh, these yeomen of England, of whom I always thought as indigenous to the soil, born there, living there, dying there, buried there, with no knowledge beyond their counted acres, but knowing those so well and thoroughly, tree by tree, crop by crop, path by path through the woodland! They have been uprooted and borne to foreign shores, but they are England, and it is for their own bit of England, weald, marsh, or fell, that they die.

'They have lived all their lives in security, and the security of centuries lies behind them, as the volume of ocean lies behind each wave that laps the shore. Now the mammoth of danger and unrest prowls round their homesteads, and a hand whose presence they did not suspect moves and removes them, pawns in the game. How can they understand? They do not. They only cling, for the sake of sanity, to what they know: their corner of England and their own individuality, rocks which have been with them since they were born, and which in the thunderstorm about their ears they can retain unaltered.

'I live amongst them now, and I know.

'I have been once in a great earthquake, and I know that the secret of its terror is that the earth, the steady immutable earth, betrays the confident footstep. So in this earthquake men cling to themselves and to their land, as they know it, as immutable things.

'I am living now in a great peace; I do not hear the din around me; I am as one in the centre of those tropical winds, where all that is in the path of the hurricane is destroyed, but in the still and silent centre birds sing and leaves do not stir. Or I am as a totally deaf man, the drums of whose ears are burst. I am happy.

'But the others, who are in the path of the wind, they are clouted and pushed and beaten, blinded and deafened by the cyclone. They are made to gyrate as the little mice were

94

made to gyrate. What is it, oh God, that drives us, poor creatures?

'I am not one of those who, at this moment, hold that the war is supreme and all-eclipsing. The war is not eternal, and its proportions are relative; only life is eternal, and fate is eternal. Fate! Do you remember the Pennistans, and how fate, the freaky humorist, played her tricks upon them? There was no escape for them then, there is no escape for us now.

'If all mankind were resigned to fate, sorrow would take wing and fly from the world.

'I think of this present stirring of nations as the stirring of huge antediluvian beasts, kicked up out of their slumber by a giant's foot, and fighting amongst themselves like the soldiers of Jason. No human eye can follow the drift of war, as no human mind can encircle the entirety of modern knowledge. We are as men in the valley, with mountains rising around, and, beyond each ridge that we climb, a farther ridge. It is for the geographers of the future to come with their maps and measure peak after peak to their correctness of altitude. And it is for us to remember that as the highest peak is as nothing upon the perfect roundness of the globe, so is our present calamity as nothing upon the perfect roundness of the scheme of destiny.'

Again that strange impulse to confide in me! in me the stranger whom he, if anything, disliked. I wondered whether our whole lives were to be punctuated by these spasmodic confidences, and whether the forging of a number of such links would finally weave together a chain of friendship? I reflected that he, the analyst, could probably explain the kink in men's brains by which confidential expansion is not necessarily based on sympathy, but I admitted to myself that I was routed by the problem.

I liked his letter; it produced in me a sensation of peace

and light, and of a great broadening. I envied him his balance and his sanity. I envy him still more now that peace has come, and that the rapid perspective of history already shows me the precision of his judgment.

I showed part of the letter to Ruth, curious to observe the impression which Malory's reflections would produce on a primitive and uncultivated brain. I knew that that letter was not the outcome of a transitory or accidental frame of mind, but that, like a rock gathering speed as it bowls down the side of a hill, the swell and rush of his considered thought had borne him along until his fingers, galloping to the dictation of his mind, had covered the sheets I now held in my hand. Ruth frankly understood no word of his letter. She merely asked me in her direct way whether I thought Mr Malory was sorry her brother-in-law had been killed. Privately I thought that some devilish cynicism in the man, some revolting sense of artistic fitness, would rejoice in a detached, inhuman fashion at the pertinence of the tragedy.

He said in his next letter to me – a reply to a letter of mine : —

'. . . Destiny and nature are, after all, the only artists of any courage, of any humour. Do they take Rawdon Westmacott? for whose disappearance all concerned must pray; no, they take Daphnis, who, of the thirty or forty million fighting men, is in the minority that should be spared.

'From the beginning they have exercised their wit on these innocent country people. How can we escape from their humour, when it gambols around us in the unseen? we cannot escape it, we can only hope to cap it with the superlative humour of our indifference.

'Around how many homes must it be gambolling now! from the little centre in the Weald of Kent, which is known to both you and me, to the little unknown centres of human life in the heart of Asia, where anxiety dwells, and where no news will ever come, but where hope will flag and droop day by day, till at last it expires in hopeless certainty.

'If you do not hear of me again, you may conclude that the arch-joker has taken me also, but remember that I shall have had the laugh on him after all, for I shall not care. However, I shall probably be spared, for no man or woman would weep for me.

'One's chief need, one's principal craving, I find, is to get Death into his true proportion. We have always been accustomed to think of Death as a suitable and even dignified ending to life in old age, but to regard the overtaking of youth by Death in quite a different light, as an unspeakable calamity. Here, of course, such an overtaking is of everyday occurrence. This, you will say, is a truism. I answer, that there is no such thing as truism in war; there is only Truth.

'If I take all my reflections about Death, slender as is their worth, and pass them through a sieve of analysis, what do I get? I get, as a dominant factor, Pity. Pity, yes, pity that these young men should have missed the good things life would have given them; not horror so much that they should be in the blackness below the ground, as pity that they should not be above it in the light. . . .'

An intense anger and irritation rose in me at his passive acceptance of what he termed fate. If man must struggle against his fellow-men in order to survive in the life-battle, then why not against fate also? He who does not resist must inevitably be crushed. It was at this stage that my great scheme began to formulate in my mind, by which I should defeat fate for the sake of Malory and Ruth; partly, largely, for the sake of their happiness, but partly also, I must admit, for the triumph of taking Malory by the hand and showing him how with the help of a little energy I had overcome the destiny he had been passively prepared to accept as inevitable. I would pit my philosophy against his philosophy, and incidentally bring two muddled lives to a satisfactory conclusion.

I hugged my scheme to myself in the succeeding months as a lunatic hugs an obsession.

I WAS a little disturbed by the thought that even I could not make myself wholly independent of what, for want of a better word, I had to call fate; independent of a certain Providence whose concurrence I daily implored, but on whose nature I deliberately tried to set a more religious complexion than did Malory, who was frankly, in every instinct, a pagan. Wriggle as I might, I could not wriggle away from the fact that as prime essentials to the success of my scheme stood the survival of Malory and the non-survival of Westmacott. If the unknown chose to thwart me in these two particulars, my cherished plan must come to naught, but a conviction, whose very intensity persuaded me of its truth, entered into my spirit that in this respect at all events all would be well.

As the war progressed I fell into one of the inconsistencies of our nature, for as the news of Malory continued good I came gradually to feel that his safety up this point was growing into a kind of earnest for his safety in the future – a conclusion in itself totally illogical – whereas the equally continued safety of Westmacott, whom I so ardently desired out of the way, distressed me not at all.

Was I presumptuous in thus constituting myself the guardian angel of two lives? I was only a poor wreck, flotsam of the war, cheated of the man's part I had hoped to play, and nursing my scheme like an old maid cheated of the woman's part she, on her side, should have played on earth.

I shall not dwell longer than I need upon the days of the war, considering them rather as an incident, a protracted incident, than as a central point in my story, for we have no need or desire to revive artificially the realities we have lived through. I quote, however, Malory on this subject:

'. . . . Our sons will scarcely be *our* children, for the war will have fathered them and mothered them both. The children of the war! growing up with the shadow of that great parent in the background of their lives, a progenitor dark as the night, yet radiant as the sun; torn with misery, yet splendid and entire with glory; poor and bereft by ruin, yet rich with gold-mines as the earth; a race of men sprung from loins broad and magnificent. They will stand like the survivors of the Flood when the waters had retreated from the clean-washed world. What will they make of their opportunity? They will not, I trust, hold up a mirror to reflect the familiar daily tragedy, but out of the depths of their own enfranchised hearts will call up a store of little, lovely, sincere, human, and simple things wherewith to make life sweet. They must be as children in a meadow. Let us have done with pretence and gloom. There is no room now in the world for the introspective melancholy of the idler. We hope for a world of active sanity.'

He reverted several times to the men who had been torn from their homes, the men who, but for war, would never have gone beyond the limit of their parish. He compared himself angrily with them, and I perceived that his theory, in embryo at Sampiero, had struck deep roots under the rain of present day realities.

'. . . I want to shout it aloud: objectivity! objectivity! action, the parent of thought. We had worn thought to a shadow, with hunting him over hill, plain, and valley. We were miners who had exhausted the drift of gold. Thank God, we are daily burying fresh gold for our successors. We were sick with the sugar of introspection; introspection, subtlest of vanities; introspection, the damnable disease. We were old and out-worn in spirit. The soil bore weakly crops, and cried out for nourishment. We are giving it blood to drink, and it grows fertile in the drinking.

'I am aware of the coarsening of my fibres; I grow more conscious of my body, less conscious of my mind. I am very humble. I know that the meanest hind who turned the ridges under the ploughshare had a truer value than I, the critic, the analyst – I use the words disparagingly – the commentator. He silently constructed while I noisily destroyed.'

Malory continued at great length in this strain, and I read between the lines of his letter that he had devoted much of the intolerable leisure of his soldier's life to the evolution of a new creed, not really new to him, for its precepts were and must always have been in his blood, but now for perhaps the first time formulated and taken close to his heart. He wrote to me more and more openly, and I knew that I was getting the expression of his inmost thoughts. I have all his letters – for they came now in numbers though with great irregularity – and have sometimes thought that I have not the right, nor he the right to compel me, to keep them to myself. As he said:

'. . . All men have creeds, and I behold myself a faddist in a universe of faddists. I cannot be wholly right, nor they wholly wrong. But I argue in my own defence, that a creed such as mine, resting on many pillars, the most mighty of which is the pillar of tolerance is at least inoffensive in a world it does not even seek to convert. I offer my little gift – and if it is rejected I withdraw my hand, and tender it elsewhere.

'I am not concerned with practical matters, nor with controversial subjects; I am not a political or a social reformer, nor a nut-eater, nor a prophet of the Pit. I am not, I fear, a very practical preacher even in my own region, for my words, were I ever to spread them abroad, could germinate only in the ready tilled field of a contented soul, and will put no bread into the mouth of the hungry. So I desist, for mere reflection is of no value in our times, and he alone has justified his existence who has relieved the poor, benefited the sickly, or fed the starving.'

I do not wholly agree with him.

At least in one particular I will take his advice, and will not dwell further upon those years. We know now that, interminable as they seemed at the time, they passed, and in a golden autumn peace came to the earth like sleep returning after night upon night of insomnia. Malory wrote to me on that occasion also, a letter more full of sarcasm, bitterness, and sorrow than any I had yet received.

'. . . So here we are at last at the end of this long, long road, more like straight railway-lines than like a road, which is a poetical thing. I look back, and I see iron everywhere: iron hurtling through the air and smashing against the soft flesh of men and the softer hearts of women; iron thundering in the sea; masonry toppling; careful labour destroyed; skies full of black smoke; giant machines. Impressionism is the only medium to express the war. In this chaos little men have laboured, trying to put their brains round the war like putting a string round the globe; and pitting their little bodies against the moving tons of iron, like a new-born baby trying to push against a Titan. What has emerged? a new, a great tradition, greater than the Trojan or the Elizabethan; a new legend for the ornament of art. For it all comes down to art in the end; the legend is greater than the fact; the mind survives the perishing matter. We are the heirs of the past. The man of action is the progenitor of the dreamer. What am I saying? The progenitor? he is the manure, merely the manure dug into the soil on which the dreamer will presently grow. Poor, inarticulate, uncomprehending men have died in their anonymous millions to furnish a song for the future singer, a vicious, invertebrate effete, no doubt; a moral hermaphrodite of a worthless generation.

'How many before me have asked, What is Truth? is it indeed a flower which blooms only on a dung-heap?

'. . . . I have seen so many men here die in their prime, who were precious to mankind or all in all to their individual loves, yet they have been taken, and I, the valueless, the solitary, am left. Is there a purpose behind these things? or am I to believe that fate is, after all, the haphazard of chance?'

We held no peace rejoicings at Pennistans', for Nancy's sake; peace was to her an additional sorrow. During the war she had had the feverish interest of having given her greatest sacrifice to the ideal of the moment, but as the horror faded away so the memory of those who had died faded also. Nancy and her kindred ceased to shine as the heroic, and became merely the unfortunate, a sad and scattered population to whom the war would last, not a few years, but all their lives. Shattered women and shattered men but to us the war appeared already as a nightmare interlude from which we had awakened.

I was now confronted with my own particular purpose, the one I had bargained with myself to carry out; I turned it over and over in my mind, and though by the light of reason I could perceive no solution to the obvious difficulty presented, yet my curious instinct persisted, that all would be well. I was certain that my purpose was a good one. I contemplated a Malory changed, softened, hardened, sobered, steadied, by the red-hot furnace of war; he had called himself an inconstant man; I felt that he would be now no longer inconstant. I contemplated a Ruth intolerant, after her four years lived in liberty, of her former bondage.

I saw them fuse, in my own mind, in mutual completion.

In the meantime, Westmacott stood ominously in the centre of the road.

I heard first of his return from Amos, as I stood with Mrs Pennistan watching the folding of the sheep. Amos had brought the sheep with him in a cart from Tonbridge market; he was taciturn while he turned them out from under the net into the hurdled fold, but when the hired man had driven away the lumbering cart, he said, jerking his thumb over his shoulder,—

'Wife, who d'you think I met on the road yonder?'

She stared at him, and he added, in his laconic way,—

'Rawdon.'

'He's back?' she said, dismayed.

Amos expanded.

'Ay. They've a system for bringing them home, it seems, according to their employ: farmers and food producers come first.'

'Then Malory,' I said involuntarily, 'will come among the last lot as a man of no occupation.'

'That'll be it. We'll be looking soon for those boys of ourn,' he said to his wife.

She smiled gladly at him, but remained pensive. Then she asked,—

'Was he alone, Amos?'

'Ay. He'd his pack on his back, too, so I doubt he'd come from the station. He'd his back to Penshurst and his face towards home. He touched his cap at me, friendly, and I twirled my whip to him, friendly, too.'

'I'm glad of that,' his wife murmured.

Amos shrugged.

'A man's glad to welcome his son-in-law back from the wars,' he said ironically as he turned to go.

Mrs Pennistan and I strolled out towards the road.

'He's dead against Rawdon; always was,' she said in a

distressed tone. 'I was for making up, and making the best of it, but Pennistan isn't that sort. He'd sooner have life unbearable than go a tittle against his prejudices. After all, Rawdon's married to Ruth, and the father of our grand-children, and there's no going against that. He's an un-accountable hard man, my man, when he chooses. I couldn't never do nothing with him, and Nancy she's the same.'

'And Mrs Westmacott?' I asked.

The distress in her tone deepened.

'I used to think Ruth a good quiet girl, but since the trick she played me over her marriage I haven't known what to think. I've lain awake o' nights worrying over it. You've heard the whole tale from Mr Malory. Gentle she was until then, and a good daughter to me, I must say, and then . . . gone in a night withouten a sign, and never a word to me in explanation since. What's a mother to make of that?'

I could have laughed at the poor woman's perplexity. I thought of the hen whose brood of ducklings takes sud-denly to the water.

'But has she never alluded to her . . . her elopement?'

'Never a word, I tell you. I asked her once, and she put on a look as black as night, and I never asked her again. I've sometimes wished Mr Malory could speak to her, I've a fancy she might answer him freer and yet I don't know.'

'I've never fully understood,' I said, wishing to make the most of my opportunity, 'whether she cares at all for her husband or not?'

'Small wonder that you haven't understood,' said Mrs Pennistan tartly, 'when her own mother is kept out in the dark. It's my belief she hates him, and its my knowledge that he ill-treats her, but at the same time it's my instinct she loves him in a way. It sounds a hard thing to say of one's child, but I've always held Ruth was a coarse, rough creature at times under her smoothness.'

She instantly repented of her words.

'There, what am I saying of my own kith and kin? I get mad when I get thinking of my girl, so you mustn't lay too much store by my talk. Pennistan'd give it me if he heard me.'

I persisted.

'Then you think that, when she ran away with him, she hated him and loved him both together?'

Mrs Pennistan paused for a long time.

'Well,' she said at last, 'if you ask me what I think, it's this. There was a deal more in that running away than any of us knew at the time. What it exactly was I don't know even now. I doubt Ruth doesn't know either, or if she does know, she doesn't own to it, not to herself even. I doubt Rawdon knows most about it.'

I saw another name becoming inevitable.

'And Mr Malory?'

She shot at me a quick suspicious look.

'You're Mr Malory's friend, what do you know?'

'I know nothing,' I said. 'He didn't know himself.'

'No,' said Mrs Pennistan suddenly, 'that's the truth. He didn't know himself. He wasn't a man to fancy those things. To me it was as plain as daylight, but Pennistan he always scoffed at me, and I daren't speak it to Ruth, and I've thought since that maybe I was wrong after all. Maybe she went with Rawdon because she loved Rawdon: maybe she didn't go, as I've sometimes thought, because she was afraid. . . . It's hard, isn't it, to see into people's hearts, even when you live in the same house with them? Day in, day out, and you know little more of them than the clothes they wear and what they like to get to eat.'

I was sorry for her. She went on,—

'Your children, they seem so close to you when they're little, they come to you when they're hungry, and they come to you when they tumble, and you cosset them; and then when they're big you find you're the last person they want

106

to come to. It's cruel hard sometimes on a woman. But they don't mean it,' she added, brightening, 'and my children have been good children to me, even Ruth.'

I met Westmacott, the formidable man, the day after his return, a Sunday, walking on the village green with his wife and the two eldest children. As I looked at him I felt a little pang of horror on realising how ardently I had desired this man to die in the trenches, and now, as he materialised for me out of a mere name into a creature of flesh and blood, I grew dismayed, and was overcome by the reality of the obstacle. Perhaps I had always unconsciously thought of him as a myth. And now here he was, and Ruth shyly introduced me.

I fancied I caught a sullen look on her face, a look of suffering, long lulled to sleep, and suddenly returned. Perhaps for the last four years he had been a myth to her also.

By his home-coming he soon waked the echoes of scandal; his way of life, they said, had not been mended by the war, and after the long restraint of discipline he broke loose into his old debauches. I noted the growing of that sullen look on Ruth's features; she made no comment, but I divined the piling-up of the thunderstorm. So, I thought, she must have looked during the month of her engagement to Leslie Dymock, when Malory in his error had considered her as a nun in her novitiate. The kettle, she had said, is long on the hob before it boils over.

She spent less time at Pennistans' than formerly, pride and obstinacy withholding all confessions from her lips or from her actions. Amos was gloomy, and Mrs Pennistan oppressed. As for me, I lived dreamily, content to let the river of events carry my boat onwards. I made no prophecies to myself, I experienced no impatience; Malory was not yet home, and I believed that by the time he got home my problem would have resolved itself automatically.

How? I never formulated, but I suppose now, looking back, that the prosaic solution of divorce lay behind my evasions. I did not take into account the dreary conventionality of the English side to Ruth's nature. People like the Pennistans do not divorce; they endure. Nor do they run away; yet Ruth had run away. Which would prove the stronger, her life-long training, or the flash of her latent blood?

There came a day – for I have dallied a long time over Malory's letters and my own reflections – when Ruth came into Pennistans' kitchen, hatless, with her three children clinging round her skirts. Her father and mother stared at her; she gave no explanation, and Amos, who was a great gentleman in his way, asked for none, and moreover checked the doleful inquiries of his wife, to whom the prompt and vulgar tear was always ready. I saw then a certain likeness between the father and the daughter; that apostolic beard of his gave him a southern dignity, and his scarlet braces marked his shirt with a blood-red slash, as red as her lips over her little teeth white as nuts. She could remain at the farm as long as she chose, he said. She had, he did not add, but his eyes added it, a refuge from all mankind in her father.

No reproaches, no recriminations, and when Mrs Pennistan, after Ruth had gone out with all apparent calm to put her children to bed, began anew to wonder tearfully what had happened, and to suggest lugubriously that as Ruth had made her bed, so she must lie on it, he checked her again and frightened her into silence by this sternness. She went out weeping, and Amos and I were left together.

I offered to go, but he assured me that my presence in the

house would be a help, adding that he supposed I had heard something of his daughter's story, and that her marriage was not a happy one. It probably cost him a great effort to say this. I tried to make it as easy as I could for him. He then asked me to remain with Ruth should her husband follow her, and should he, Amos, or one of her brothers, not be in the house.

I could see that he thought it likely that Westmacott would come over sooner or later.

I was greatly elated at the turn things had taken, and felt that my belief in the lucky star of my scheme had been justified. I had no doubt now that Ruth would rid herself of Westmacott, and do for herself what the war had not done for her. I hung about the farm all day, partly to oblige Amos, who had his usual work to attend to, but principally to satisfy the tense spirit of expectation which had risen in me since the morning. As the player sees an imaginary line running between his ball and the objective, so I imagined a string running between the moment at Sampiero when Mallory had said. 'Do you know the Weald of Kent?' and this moment when I, a tardy, but, I flattered myself, an essential actor, waited about Pennistans' threshold for the advent of Rawdon Westmacott. All the beads but one were now threaded on that string I must watch the last and final threading, before I could put on the clasp.

Towards evening I espied Westmacott entering a distant field, and something in me gave a fierce leap of exultation. I then realised the practical difficulties of the position. Here was I, left on guard, but physically quite unable to grapple with the wiry man should he lay hands on me, or on his wife. I thought for an instant of summoning Amos, but as instantly rejected the idea: the final act must lie between Westmacott, Ruth, and myself. Had I been alone, I would have chanced his violence; as it was, I must consider the woman. I ran quickly into the house, up to my room, and brought down my service revolver.

When I came into the kitchen carrying this weapon, Ruth, who was sitting there sewing, as placidly, I swear, as she had sat sewing in her own kitchen the first time I had seen her, looked at my loaded hand and up into my face with a grave, inquiring surprise. I reassured her. Her husband, I told her, was coming across the fields and would doubtless insist on seeing her, and considering the nature of the man I had thought it best to have an unanswerable threat ready to hand. With that muzzle we would keep him at bay.

Ruth rose very quietly and took the weapon from me. I had no idea of resistance. Malory himself could not have felt more definitely than I that the words we were to speak, the actions we were to perform, were already written out on a slowly unwinding scroll.

She asked me to leave her alone with her husband; to my feeble protest, made by my tongue, but barely seconded by the vital part of my being, the part so intensely conscious, yet at the same time so pervaded by a sense of trance and un-reality, – to that feeble protest she replied, bitterly enough that she had faced him many times before and with my weapon on the table beside her would face him with additional confidence and security. She had already taken it from me, and now laid it on the table, speaking as one does to a child from whom one has just taken a dangerous toy. She smiled as she spoke, so serenely that I felt sure she had accepted the revolver merely for the sake of my peace of mind. She charged me to keep the children away, should I see them drawing near to the house, and with that injunction she took me kindly by the shoulders and turned me out into the garden.

Westmacott entered it at the same moment by the swing-gate. His looks were black as he passed me and strode into the house he had not darkened since his marriage. I stood

110

out in the garden alone in the dusk. I looked in through the latticed window of the kitchen, seeing every detail as the detail of a Dutch picture, lit by the fire; the window was very largely blocked by the red geraniums, but I could see the deal table, the swinging lamp, the brass ornaments gleaming by the fireplace, the pictures on the walls, the thin ribbon of steam coming from the spout of the singing kettle; I could even see the brown grain in the wood of which the table-top was made. I saw Ruth standing, and Westmacott looking at her; then he caught sight of me, and with an angry gesture dragged the curtain across the window.

I was now shut out from all participation in this act of the drama, but I did not care; I felt that what must be, must be, that the inevitable was right, and, above all, ordained. Come what might, no human agency could interfere. I smiled to myself as I thought of Malory's triumph could he behold my resignation, and as I smiled I felt Malory's presence in the garden, waiting like me, and, like me, entirely passive. I saw his face; his iron gray hair where it grew back from his temples; I saw the tiny hairs in his nostrils, and the minute pores of his skin. My head was swimming, and the vividness of my perception stabbed me.

Then a little scent floated out to me, and I wondered vaguely what it was, and what were the memories it awakened, and in some dim, extremely complicated way I knew those memories were awakened by a mental rather than a physical process, and that they were, at best, only second-hand. A narrow street, yoked bullocks, and the clamour of a Latin city. . . . These meaningless and irrelevant words shaped themselves out of the mist of my sensitiveness. I linked them and the picture they created to the violence of feeling within the little room behind the drawn curtain, and as I did so they fell away together from the twilit English garden, the English country; fell away to their own place, as a thing apart; or shall I say, they stood behind

111

the English country as a ghostly stranger behind a familiar form? This was the ghost of which Malory had always been conscious. Then I knew that my troubled perplexity was but the echo of Malory's first perplexity, and I narrowed it down with an effort of will to the scent of roasting chestnuts. The ancient woman in her bedroom was at her usual occupation.

I folded my arms and leant my back against the house wall; I heard the rise and fall of angry voices within the room; I found that I could look only at little things, such as the cracks in the stone paving of the garden path, or the latch on the gate, and that the horizon, when I raised my eyes towards it, swam. I tried to drag back my failing sense of proportions. As I did this, clinging on to and deliberately ranging my thoughts in ordered formation, there emerged the dearness and all-eclipsing importance of my scheme to me in the past; I realised that never for a moment had it been absent from my conscious or my sub-conscious thought. So, I said to myself, this is the phenomenon of poets, and are they, I wonder, as passive as I am when after months of carrying their purpose in their brain, the moment comes of its fruition? Have they, like me, no feeling of control? I remembered what Malory had said of the co-relation of human effort.

I looked towards the darkened window and, hearing the drone of voices, beheld myself again as the brother of the poet whose puppets, brought by him to a certain point, continue to work along the lines he has laid down, as though independent of his agency. I would resume control, I thought, when this so terribly inevitable act had played itself out. Then I would step in, lead Malory to Ruth, and again step out, leaving them to the joy of their bewilderment.

Why should I have cherished this scheme so passionately? so passionately that my desire had risen above my reason, carrying with it that strange conviction that by the sheer force of my will events would shape themselves – as indeed they were shaping – under my inactive hand? Why? I could not explain, but as the twilight deepened rapidly in the garden I saw again Malory's grave, lean face, heard his half-sad, half-happy comments, was pierced by the pitiable and unnecessary tragedy of his loneliness – Malory away in France, unconscious of the intensity of the situation created around him, without his knowledge and without his consent, by a woman who loved him and a man who, I suppose, loved him too.

It was at that moment, when I had worked myself up into a positive exaltation, that I heard a sudden angry shout and a shot from a revolver.

I awoke, and I confess that before rushing into the house I stood for a dizzy second while a thousand impressions wheeled like a flock of startled birds in my brain. It was over, then? Westmacott was dead, I was sure of that. Would the mice, two miles away, be waltzing? I had an insane desire to run over and look. Westmacott was dead; then I had killed him, I was his murderer as much as if I stood in Ruth's place with the smoking revolver in my hand. It was over; the recent tradition of war, where life was cheap, had joined with Concha's legacy for the fulfilment of my purpose. What a heritage! for that double heritage, not fate, had helped me out. Blood, war, and I were fellow conspirators.

I stood for a second only before I burst open the door, but the strength of my impression was already so powerfully upon me that when I saw Westmacott by the fire holding the revolver I did not believe my eyes. When I say I did not believe my eyes I mean that I was quite soberly, deliberately persuaded that my eyes were telling an actual falsehood to my brain. Westmacott could not be standing by the fire; he must be lying somewhere on the ground, huddled and lifeless. I removed my eyes from the false

Westmacott standing by the fire, and sent them roving over the floor in search of that other Westmacott from whom life had flown.

I ran my eyes up and down the cracks between the tiles until they came to a darkness, and then, running them upwards, I reached the face of Ruth. She was there, shrinking as she must suddenly have shrunk when he snatched the revolver from her. In her face I read defeat, reaction, submission. She had struck her blow, and it had failed; and she and I were together beaten and vanquished.

I knew that my attempt would be hopeless, but a great desperation seized hold of me, and I cried out, absurdly, miserably,—

'There are other methods.'

She only shook her head, and, pointing at the revolver, said,—

'It kicked in my hand.'

I looked across the room and running to the fire I picked up some bits of china which had fallen in the grate; I tried to fit them together, repeating sorrowfully,—

'Look, you have broken a plate, you have broken a plate to pieces.'

V

For how long we stood gazing at those ironical shards I do not know. There are moments of suspension in life when the whirling mind travels at so great a rate that everything else seems stationary; so, now, we were touched into immobility while our minds flew forward into space and time. I cannot say what the others found in that fourth dimension of thought; I, personally, returned to earth utterly inarticulate, with these two words shaping themselves and singing over and over in my brain: Futile creatures! futile creatures! It was as though some little mocking demon sat astride my nerve cords, drumming his heels, and chanting his refrain. I could have shaken myself like a dog coming out of water to shake him off. Then I became aware of Westmacott's voice speaking at an immense distance.

He must have been speaking for some time before the sound pierced through to my ears, for I saw Ruth moving in obedience to his voice before I had grasped what he was saying. Her movement made the same impression upon me as his voice: muffled, slow, and infinitely remote; she crept, rather than she walked, and when she raised her hand she raised it with such torpid and deliberate effort that she seemed to be dragging it upwards with some heavy weight attached. As for her feet, they positively stuck to the ground. Westmacott said something more; he pointed. She turned, still with that slow laborious deliberation, and moved like a shackled ghost from the room.

Westmacott and I were left, and we were silent, he perhaps from choice, I certainly from inability to speak. I think now that he was less shattered than Ruth or me, having played a more negative rôle; he had merely stood there to be shot at, while Ruth and I had flung, she direct, I indirect, passion into the shooting. We were worn, spent, exhausted, he had his forces still intact. An absurd phrase came into my mind, so childish that I hesitate to write it down: Which would you rather be, the shooter or the shootee? and presently I hit on the rhyme, so that a sing-song began in my head:

'Which would you rather be,
The shooter or the shootee?'

and still Westmacott stood there holding the revolver, and I stood there holding the pieces of the broken plate, and all the while I seemed to hear the corner-stones of my cherished schemes dropping to earth like pieces of masonry after an explosion. We stood quite motionless. Overhead somebody was moving about. Outside it was nearly dark.

Perception was beginning to return to me, bringing in its train a sense of defeat. I had often wondered how the people in a play or in a story continued to live their lives after the climax which parted spectator and actor for ever, I had often followed them in spirit, come down to breakfast with them next morning, so to speak, producing the situation into the region of inevitable anti-climax. Here I was, then, at the old game, an actor myself. I supposed that the play was at an end, and that this was the return to life. That the play should end happily or unhappily, was an accident proper to the play only; all that was certain, all that was inevitable, was that life must be gone on with after the play was over. You couldn't stop; you were like a man tied on to the back of a traction-engine, willy-nilly you had to go on walking, walking, walking. The dreariness of it! I looked at the pieces of broken plate in my hand, the sum total of all that passion, all that great outburst of pent emotion. I threw back my head, and laughed long, loud, and bitterly.

Westmacott regarded me without surprise, scarcely with

116

interest. He appeared cold and quite indifferent, entirely in possession of his faculties. I grew ashamed under his dispassionate gaze, my laughter ceased, and I laid the pieces of plate on the table. Then it occurred to me we were waiting for something. The movement overhead had died away, but as I listened I heard steps upon the stair, several sets of steps, light pattering steps as of children, and heavier steps, as of a grown person.

Then Westmacott stirred; he went across the room and opened the door. I saw Ruth standing in the passage with her children. She was hatless as she had arrived, but the glow of the lamp, hanging suspended from the ceiling, where it fell upon the curve of her little head, drew a line of light as upon a chestnut. Westmacott nodded curtly, passed out, and his family followed him in a passive and mournful procession.

I watched them go, across the little garden, through the swing-gate, and into the dusky fields beyond. They seemed to me infinitely gray, infinitely dreary, infinitely broken, the personages of a flat and faded fresco. All that pulsating passion had passed, like an allegory of life, leaving only death behind. Gone was the vital flame from the human clay. And nothing had come of it, nothing but a broken plate. What ever comes of men's efforts, I thought bitterly? so little, that we ought to take for our criterion of success, not the tangible result, but the intangible ardour by which the attempt is prompted. So rarely is the one the gauge of the other! I looked again at the little train rapidly disappearing into the darkness, a funeral cortège, carrying with it the corpse of slain rebellion. I saw the years of their future, a vista so stark, so arid, that I physically recoiled from its contemplation. How hideous would be the existence of those children, suffering perpetually from a constraint they could not explain, a constraint which lacked even to the elements of terror, so dead a thing was it, in which terror, a lively, vivid reality, could find no place. Death and stagnation would be their lot.

The darkness of the fields had now completely swallowed them up, but I still stood looking at the spot where I had last seen them, and saying a final good-bye to the tale that place had unfolded to me. This time, I was certain, no sequel was still to come. On the morrow I should leave the Pennistans' roof, with no hope that an echo of the strangely cursed, ill-fated, unconscious family would ever reach me again in the outer world.

A peace so profound as to be almost unnatural had settled over the land, one or two stars had come out, and I wondered vaguely why Amos and his people had not yet returned home from work. I supposed that they were making the most of a fine evening. The Pennistans would accept their daughter's defeat, I was sure, with the usual stoic indifference of the poor. At last I turned slowly in the doorway, a great melancholy soaking like dew into my bones, so that I fancied I felt the physical ache.

Now I have but the one concluding incident to tell, before I have done with this portion of my cumbersome, disjointed story, an incident which has since appeared to me frightening in its appositeness, as though deliberately planned by some diabolically finished artist as a rounding of the whole. Malory had spoken of destiny and nature as being the only artists of any humour or courage, and upon my soul I am tempted to agree with him when I think over the events of that packed evening, of which I was the sole and baffled spectator. I said this incident appeared to me frightening; I repeat that statement, for I can conceive of no situation more frightening than for a man to find himself and other human beings shoved hither and thither by events over which he has no control whatsoever, the conduct of life taken entirely out of his hands, especially a man who, like me, had always struggled resentfully against the imposition of fate on free-will, but never more so than in the past few weeks. Wherever I turned that night, mockery was there ready to greet me.

I went again, as I have said, into the house with the intention of waiting in the kitchen on Amos's return. In this small plan as in my larger ones I was, it appeared, to be thwarted, for as I passed down the narrow passage I noticed that the door of old Mrs Pennistan's rooms was open. I paused at first with no thought of alarm. I longed to go in, and to tell the ancient woman of the futile suffering she had brought upon her hapless descendants. I longed insanely to shout it into her brain and to see remorse wake to life in her faded eyes. As I stood near her door she grew for me into a huge, portentous figure, she and her love for Oliver Pennistan, and I saw her, the tiny woman I had all but forgotten, as a consciously evil spirit, a malign influence, the spring from which all this river of sorrow had flowed. Then my steps were drawn nearer and nearer to the door, till I stood at last on the threshold, looking for the first time into the room. Some one, presumably the now invisible servant, had lit the two candles on the dressing-table, and these with the glow of the fire between the bars threw over the room a fitful light. I had, curiously enough, no sense of intrusion; I might have been looking at a mummy. Yet I should have remembered that the occupant was not a mummy, for the familiar smell of the chestnuts had greeted me even in the passage.

She was sitting in her usual place over the fire, her back turned to me, and a black shawl tightly drawn round her shrunken shoulders. Again I was struck by her look of fragility. I had a sudden impulse that I would speak to her, and would try to draw some kind of farewell from her, explaining that I was leaving the house the next day – though whether she had ever realised my presence there at all I very much doubted.

As I went forward the crackle of a chestnut broke the utter stillness of the room. I waited for her to pick it out of the grate with the tongs, but she did not stir. I came softly round her chair and stood there, waiting for her to notice me, as I had seen the Pennistans do when they did not wish to startle her. Indeed, so tiny and frail was she, that I thought a sudden fright might shatter her, as too loud a noise will kill a lark.

I looked down at the chestnuts on the bar, and then I saw that they were quite black. I bent down. They were burnt black and friable as cinders. Sudden panic rushed over me. I dropped on to my knees and stared up into the old woman's fallen face. She was dead.

PART III

I

DURING ten years my story remained at that, with a fictitious appearance of completion. Then I received a letter which, without further preamble, I here transcribe:

'. . . I laugh to myself when I think of you receiving this letter, surely the most formidable letter ever penned by mortal man to mortal man, a letter one hundred and fifty pages long; who ever heard of such a thing? You will stare dismayed at the bundle, and, having forgotten the sight of my writing, will turn to the end for the signature; which finding, you will continue to stare bewildered at the name of Malory until light breaks upon you as faint and feeble as a winter dawn. Let me help you by reminding you of Sampiero first, and of Pennistan's farm later. You see, I am not vain, and am perfectly prepared to believe that the little set of your fellow-men among whom I figured had entirely faded from your mind.

'Are they gradually reviving as I write? and do you, as they one by one sit up in the coffins to which you had prematurely relegated them, greet them with a smile? Oh, I don't blame you, my dear fellow, for having put us away, myself included, in those premature graves. I should have done as much myself. I will go further: I should have buried the lot that day I left you at Sampiero; yes, I am sure I should not have displayed your energy in seeking out the birds in their very nest.

'I had better warn you at the start that you will find it hard to believe the things I am going to tell you. You know

121

already of two crises in the lives of my Hispano-Kentish yeomen, two crises which I think have puzzled you sufficiently – though in the first case I suspect that you were more clear-sighted than I – but in this third crisis with which I deal you will probably refuse to believe altogether. I do not pretend to explain it myself. I only know that it happened, and therefore that it is true. Were it not true, I would not dare to foist its relation on any living man, however credulous. Human ingenuity could not, however, have planned this sequel, nor human courage have invented a solution at once so subtle and so naïf, and so in the absurd incredibility of my tale I place my reliance that it will carry conviction.

'Ours has been a queer friendship, but one which has held great value for me; I think many people would be the better for such a friendship in their lives. Of course, to make it ideal, I should never have seen you; picked your name and address out of a telephone directory, and written; I am sure you would have answered. Then I should have had no reserve towards you, not that I have much now, but you see I never can be certain that I am not going to meet you in a train or in the street, when my ideally unknown correspondent and I could pass by without recognition, but when you and I would have to stop, and shake hands, and a host of intimate, remembered phrases would come crowding up to people our silence. I dislike such embarrassments. I find that solitude, like leprosy, grows upon one with age, for I observe myself physically wincing from the idea that I might possibly meet you as I have said, in a train or in the street.

'You will be surprised, after this, to hear that I no longer live alone. But I shall not give you the pleasure of anticipating the end of what I have set out to tell you; I am going to roll my story off my pen for my own delectation far more than for yours, and to see whether in the telling I cannot chance upon the explanation of various points which are still obscure.

'I was never a man who thought life simple; I had not a five-hundred word vocabulary wherewith I explained the primitive emotions of birth, hunger, adolescence, love, and death; no, life was always difficult and involved to me, but now in the evening of my own existence, serene and ordered as that evening turns out to be, it appears as a labyrinth beyond conception, with not one, but a thousand centres into which we successively stray. Difficult, difficult and heavy to shift are the blocks of which our mansion is built. Nor am I now speaking of social-political creeds which are to govern the world; I am speaking only of poor, elementary human beings, for, not having mastered the individual, I don't attempt to discuss the system under which he lives. Big and little things alike go to our building; and if it was the war which first put the grace of humility into me, it is the sequel to a tale of plain people which has kept it there.

'Oh, the humility of me! I cross my arms over my eyes and bow myself down to the ground like a Mussulman at prayer. There's nothing like life for teaching humility to a man, nothing like life for shouting "Fool! fool! fool!" at him till he puts his hands over his ears. It buzzes round our heads like a mosquito inside mosquito-curtains. Humility isn't the gift of youth – thank God – for it takes a deal of buffeting to drive it into us. The war should have taught us a lesson in humility; a wider lesson, I mean, than the accident of defeat or victory, efficiency or non-efficiency. Let us ignore those superficial aspects of the war. What we are concerned with, is the underlying forces, the courage, the endurance, the loyalty, the development of a great heart by little mean men; all this, abstract but undeniable, unrivalled, the broadest river of human excellence that ever flowed. What then? Mistaken, by God! wrong-headed! an immense sacrifice on the altar of Truth which was all the time the altar

123

of Untruth. Doesn't it make you weep? All the gold of the human heart poured out, like the gold of the common coffers, in a mistaken cause. It's barbaric; it's more than barbaric, it's pre-historic; it's going back to the Stone Age. We can't say these things now; not yet; not from lack of courage, but from a sense of tact: we're living in the wrong century. It's an outrage on tact to say to your century what will be self-evident to the next; therefore we continue to hate our enemy and love our country; mistaken ideals both.

'There, my dear fellow, I profoundly apologise; if I oughtn't to say these things to my century I oughtn't to say them to you either, not that you are narrow enough to condemn me, but because I shall bore you. I promised you, too, that my letter was to deal with our little corner of Kent, and on that understanding I have induced you to read thus far. I reflect, moreover, that I have no right to speak thus and thus to a man who has lost much of his activity in his country's service. Mrs Pennistan has drawn me a touching picture of you, though she hasn't much descriptive talent, has she? A motherly soul, pathetically out of place among that untamed brood. Like the majority of people, she lives a life of externals, with sentimentality as a mild substitute for the more heroic things, and it has been her misfortune for her lot to fall among people who, in the critical moments of their lives, allow themselves to be guided by internal powers of which Mrs Pennistan knows nothing. I said, nothing. Yet is such true placidity possible? When you see a person, a body, marvellous casket and mask of secrets, what do you think? I think, there stands a figure labelled with a name, but he, or she, has lived a certain number of years; that is to say, has suffered, rejoiced, loved, been afraid, known pain; owns secrets, some dirty, some natural, some shameful, some merely pathetic; and the older the figure, the greater my wonderment and my admiration. Mrs Pennistan, dull, commonplace woman, once gave herself to Amos; was then that not an immortal moment? But if she remembers at all, she remembers without imagination; she can't touch her recollection into life.

'And she dwells among hot, smouldering natures to whom the life of the spirit is real. She doesn't understand them, and when her daughter, who is apparently living in externals likewise, breaks out into the unexpected, she is perplexed, dismayed, aggrieved. She doesn't travel on parallel lines with the workings of such a mind as her daughter's and consequently has to catch up with a sudden leap forward which disturbs her comfortable amble. She had to take such a leap when her daughter eloped, and another similar leap when her daughter tried to shoot her son-in-law. Humorous, isn't it? and rather sad. I feel less for Amos, whose instinct is more in tune with Ruth's, and is able to follow quickly by instinct if not by reason.

'At present Mrs Pennistan's mind must be in chaos, but it is happy chaos, and so she accepts it without disproportionate bewilderment. Besides, she has come by now to a fortunate state of resignation, in which she is determined to be surprised at nothing. I have questioned her on the subject. She is so profoundly unanalytical that I had some difficulty in getting her to understand at all what I was driving at, let alone getting her to answer my questions; still, what she told me was, in substance, this:

' "Ruth was my own girl, and a quiet girl at that, but Rawdon isn't my boy, and we all knew that Rawdon was queer (this is the adjective she invariably applies, I find, to anything a little bit beyond her), so we got into the way of not being surprised when Rawdon did queer things. Though, I must say, this beats all. After ten years! . . . And he no coward either, I'll say that for him. He was always a reckless boy, and if you'd seen the things he did you'd wonder, like I do, that he ever lived to grow up."

'That, of course, is where her lack of imagination leaves

her so much at fault. She has seen Rawdon climb into the tops of spindly trees after jackdaws' nests, and has trembled lest he should fall and break his head, and has marvelled at his daring; but she cannot imagine, because she cannot with her physical eyes behold the torments he endured of late because his moral imaginative cowardice was so much greater than his physical courage. She cannot understand that the force of his imagination was such as to drive him away from all that he most desired. She cannot understand this, and I will admit that for us, who are phlegmatic English folk, it is difficult to understand also. We must dismiss our own standards first, and approach the situation with an unbiased eye. We must, in fact, pull prejudice down from his throne and set up imagination in his place. We must forget our training and our national conventions, if we wish to understand something alien to ourselves, something alien, but not thereby impossible or, believe me, uninteresting.

'I look back over what I have already written, and am bound to confess that I have set down hitherto the incoherent thoughts that came into my head, simply because I have been afraid of tackling my settled duty. To deal with ten years – for it is now ten years since the period of our correspondence ceased with the ceasing of the war – is a very alarming task for any man to undertake. I could, of course, acquaint you in a dozen lines with the salient happenings of those years. But it amuses me to cast them into the form of a narrative, and you will forgive me if I should slip into elaborating scenes in which I played no part.

'At the end of the war, I must tell you, I came back to England with no very fixed ideas as to my future. I had been a wanderer, and, I say it with shame, a dilettante all my life, and I felt that my restlessness had not yet spent itself. I had hated, oh, how I had hated, the discipline of the army! I had no joy in war; my theories – I can't call them prin-

ciples, for they were things too fluid for so imposing a name
– my theories were in complete disaccord with war, and
moreover my freedom, for the love of which I had sacrificed a possible home and children, was now taken from
me, and, in its place, fetters both physical and moral were
clamped upon me. As my feet had to move left! right! left!
right! so my poor rebellious tongue had to move left! right!
also. And yet, there were fine moments in that war; one
learnt lessons, and one watched great splendid fountains
leaping upwards out of the sea of humanity. . . . Then the
end came when I was free, and could make a bonfire of my
uniform. I wondered what I should do next, and as I wondered I became aware of two things pulling at me; one thing
pulled me towards the Weald of Kent, and the other pulled
me towards the Channel, where all the world would lie open
to my wandering. I decided that the two were, in order,
compatible.

'What a free man I was! I enjoyed paying the full fare for
my ticket, and no longer travelling by warrant. You and I
both know that journey to Penshurst, but you don't know
the freedom that was mine in those fields; I shouted, I ran,
I jumped the brooks, I was like a lamb in May, forgetful of
my middle-age. And then I was suddenly lonely, wanting,
for the first time in my life, a companion to share my light-
heartedness. I wished that you were with me, for I couldn't
think of anybody else. Home from the war; free indeed, but
no welcome anywhere. Not even a dog. And as for a
woman! . . .

'Westmacott had come home, and I knew that he had
found his children grown, and his wife, perhaps, temporarily
happy to see him. At least he could turn to watch her
beauty as she slept. . . . I cursed my instinct for following
people into their private lives, a damnable trick, and nothing
more than a trick, but one which made me lower my eyes in
shame when next I met them. Peeping through keyholes. I

had done it all my life. Well, if anybody peeped through my keyhole, there wouldn't be much to see.

'How queerly things work out sometimes, for no sooner had I emerged from the fields on to the cross-roads, where the finger-post says "Edenbridge, Leigh, Cowden," still wrapped in my loneliness as in a cloak, I came upon Mrs Pennistan walking slowly up and down, waiting, I presumed, for Amos. At the sight of me she stopped and stared, till we simultaneously cried one another's names. I was filled with real warm gladness on seeing her there unchanged, unchangeable, and I went forward with my hands outstretched to clasp her fat, soft hands – do you remember her hands? they spoke of innumerable kneadings of dough, and she had no knuckles, only dimples where the knuckles should have been. And then, before I knew what had happened, that good woman's arms were round my neck and her soft, jolly face was against mine, and she kissed me and I kissed her, and I swear there were tears in her eyes, which, for that matter, she didn't trouble to conceal.

'Presently Amos came along. I had intended returning to London that night, but they would hear nothing of it, and I found myself supping as of old in their happy kitchen, and going upstairs later to that bare little room which had once been mine and had since been yours. It is a real satisfaction to me that you should be as familiar with these surroundings as I am myself, for you have, as you read, the same picture as I have as I write, and this harmony we could never achieve were I telling you of places and faces you had never seen.

'We talked, naturally, of you, for after the manner of old friends we travelled from one to the other of persons we had known. The sons, who were there solemnly munching, lent a certain constraint to the evening. And I missed so poignantly, so unexpectedly, the figure of the old woman by the fire. I had not realised until then what a prominent figure it had been, although so tiny and so silent, bent over the eternal chestnuts, the great-great grandmother of the little Westmacotts. Will you smile if I tell you that I took the diary up to bed with me, and read myself again into the underworld of Spain?

'Was it you, by the way, that drew a charcoal portrait of me over the wash-stand in my room?

'I got up and dressed the next morning still uncertain as to whether I should or should not go over to Westmacotts'. I do not exactly know why I was uncertain, but perhaps my loneliness on the previous day had more to do with it than my self-offered pretext, that my acquaintance with Ruth had better be left where it was at our last meeting. Remember, I had not seen her since she stood distraught but resolute in the cowshed with the Hunter's moon as a halo behind her head. What could one say to people in greeting when one's last words had been full of dark mystery and of things which don't come very often to the surface of life? In a word, I was afraid. Afraid of embarrassment, afraid of the comfort of her home, afraid of her. Afraid of my own self as a companion through lonely years afterwards. I dressed very slowly because I wanted to put off the inevitable moment of making up my mind. And after all it was Mrs Pennistan who made it up for me, for such was her surprise when I mentioned catching a train which would certainly leave me no time for the visit, that I said I would go.

'I realised then that I was glad. When I was a boy and couldn't make up my mind whether I wanted to do a thing or not, I used to toss a coin, not necessarily abiding by the coin's decision, but my own predominant feeling of relief or disappointment. I found the system invaluable. In this case Mrs Pennistan had spun herself as a coin for me.

'Westmacott, I knew, would be out. Would Ruth be out, too? and my problem thus re-solved by, as it were, another spin of the coin? She was not out; she was in her kitchen rolling a white paste with a rolling-pin, the sleeves of her blue linen dress turned back, and as she rolled she sang to the baby which lay in a low cradle in the corner. The baby lay on its back waving a piece of red coral which it occasionally chewed. I stood for quite a long time in the doorway watching them, and then Ruth looked up and saw me.

'I suppose I had remembered her blush as the most vivid thing about her, for I had waited there fully expecting her to look up and colour as she always did when surprised in any way, but instead of this she stood there gazing at me with the colour faded entirely from her face. She stood holding the rolling-pin, as white as the flour upon her hands and arms. The strong light of the window was upon her. Red geraniums were in the window. The strident voice of a canary broke our stillness.

'"Ruth," I said, "aren't you glad to see me?"

'I went forward into the kitchen, standing close to her by the table, and light was all around us, light, and the song of the bird. Everything was light, white, and dazzling; a flood of light, and bright colours. Revelation, like an archangel, was in that room.

'She asked,—

'"Where have you come from?"

'"From your father's house."

'"You're living there?"

'"Only for to-day."

'"And then you're going . . .?"

'"Away."

'"Away?"

'"Yes."

'"For good?"

'"To travel . . ."

'I saw her face, and her beauty began to swim in front of my eyes, and a roaring began in my ears like a man who is

130

breathing chloroform. Swimming, swimming, all the room and the light, and I heard my own voice as I had never heard it before,—

' "Ruth! Ruth! you must come with me."

' "Come with you?"

' "Yes, now, at once. Before your husband comes back. Get your things. I give you five minutes."

'She cried,—

' "Oh, but the baby?"

' "I'll look after it while you go upstairs."

' "No, no," she said, "not now; afterwards?"

'I understood.

' "Take it with you."

' "But, my dear, I've three children!"

'The divinity was vanishing from the room, the sunlight grew flat and cold. We stared at one another. I heard Westmacott's voice out in the yard. I said desperately,—

' "Let me tell him!"

' "Oh, no!" she cried shrinking, "no, no, no."

' "You're afraid," I taunted her.

' "What if I am? Please go."

' "Alone?"

' "Please, please go."

II

'You want to know if I went? I did, and in the yard I met Westmacott, who discussed with me the prospects of the season. He was particularly affable, and I did my utmost not to appear absent-minded. I suppose that I succeeded, for his affability increased, culminating in an invitation to join him in a glass of ale within the house. I was dismayed, and protested that I had no time, also – quite untruthfully – that since the war I had given up drink of all kinds. He urged me.

' "You'll not refuse to taste my wife's cider?"

'I thought that I cried out,—

' "Man alive, I come straight from imploring your wife to come away with me," but as his expression remained the same, and neither glazed into horror nor blazed into fury, I suppose that the words, though they screamed in my head, never materialised on my lips.

'I was helpless. He led me back, odious and hospitable, into the kitchen where Ruth still stood rhythmically rolling the dough. The sun had gone behind a cloud, and the room, which had been so dazzling with its colours and its clarity, was dim, even to the red of the geraniums, even to the glow under the skin of Ruth. Dead, I thought, dead, dead.

'Westmacott stood outside, stamping the clay from his boots, and calling to his wife for cider. I winced from his heartiness, and from the tragic absurdity of my position. If only tragedy could be our lot, we should at least enjoy the consolation of the heroic, but in the comic tragedy to which Providence so delights in exposing us, there is no consolation. I was thankful that Westmacott did not know what a fool he was successfully making of me.

'Ruth took down from the dresser an earthenware jug,

and went through into the little back hall of the place. I watched her through the door which she had left open. She filled the jug at a great wooden barrel; the golden cider streamed out from the tap, and she held the jug with a precision and a steadiness of hand that made me marvel. Returning, she set it with two glasses on the table.

' "This is my own brewing," she said to me.

'I thought that the cider must surely spill from my glass as I raised it from the table, or that it must bubble and choke in my throat as I drank with her eyes upon me. I felt trapped and prisoned, but in Westmacott's face there was nothing sinister, no trace of suspicion. He was not playing a game with me. Perversely enough, I should have preferred an outburst of fury on his part, to have felt his fist in my face, and to roll with him, body grappling with body, on the floor. But this could not be, and I must sit, drinking cider, between those two, a husband and wife whom the flash of a revolver had so nearly separated not many weeks beforehand, a revolver fired in anger and hatred, and in a desire for freedom; I must sit there, near a woman between whom and myself unforgettable words had been suddenly illuminatingly spoken. I laughed; Westmacott had just made some remark to which my laugh came as an inappropriate answer; he looked a little surprised, and I was hunting about for some phrase to cover my lapse, when Ruth said,—

' "Here are the boys."

'They came in whistling, but fell silent as they saw me, and took their caps off awkwardly. They were good-looking little boys – but I forget: you've seen them. Westmacott glanced at them with obvious pride. Ruth moved with her former steadiness to the cupboard to cut them each a chunk of bread liberally spread with jam; she pushed their chairs close up to the table, and ran her fingers through their rough mops of hair. They began to eat solidly. Westmacott winked at me.

' "There's a mother for you," he said.

'I could make no reply to his hideous jocularity; if I had spoken, I should have screamed.

'I felt that I should never escape, that the situation would last for ever. I was, naturally enough, not very clear in my mind just then, but already I seemed to see my recent scene with Ruth as a sunlit peak bursting out of the dreariness and blindness of days, as brief as the tick of a clock, but as vibrant as a trumpet-call, while the present scene was long, interminable, flat as a level plain. Yes, that was my impression: the peak and the plain. I longed to get away, that I might dwell at my leisure upon that moment full of wonder. I bitterly resented my bondage. I wanted to go away by myself to some solitary corner where I might sit and brood for hours over the one moment in which, after years of mere vegetation, I could tell myself that I had truly lived. I felt that every minute by which my stay in that kitchen was prolonged, was making of the place a thing of nightmare, instead of the enchanted chamber it actually was, and this also I resented. Why could not I have come, lived my brief spell, and gone with an untarnished treasure imprisoned for ever within my heart? Why should perfection be marred by the clumsiness of a farmer's hospitality?

'Nor was this all. Creeping over me came again the humiliating sensation which I had more than once experienced in the presence of Ruth and Westmacott, the sensation that they were alien to me, bound together by some tie more mysterious than mere cousinship, a tie which, I believed, held them joined in spite of the hatred that existed between them. I won't go into this now. It is a mystery which lies at the very foot of their strange relationship. I do not suppose that Ruth was conscious of it – she was, after all, an essentially unanalytical and primitive creature – but it drove her now to a manifestation as typical of her in particular as it was of all women in general.

'She set herself deliberately to increase my misery and discomfort by every trick within her power. She must have been aware of what I was enduring, and you would have thought, however indifferent to me in the emotional sense, that she would have tried, in ordinary human pity and charity, to help me to escape as soon as possible from my wretched position, and to make that position less wretched while it still lasted. You would have thought this. Any man would have thought it. But apparently women are different.

'She took, then, my misery and played with it, setting herself to intensify it by every ruse at her disposal. She contrived, with diabolical subtlety, to separate us into two groups, one consisting of herself, her husband, and her children, the other consisting of me, isolated and alone. To this day I do not know whether she wanted to punish me for my former temerity, or whether she was simply obeying some obscure feminine instinct. In any case, she succeeded. I had never felt myself such an intruder. Even the resemblance between husband and wife, the curious, intangible resemblance of race and family in their dark looks, rose up and jeered at me. "We understand one another," something seemed to say, "and we are laughing together at your expense."

'I realised then that the calm with which she had received me, and had drawn my cider, the matter-of-fact way in which she had told me it was of her own brewing, were all part of her scheme, as was her present conversation, standing by the table, and her occasional demonstrations of affection towards her boys. You will remember perhaps that I once told you of a walk she and I had taken to Penshurst. Well, I dimly felt that her behaviour on that occasion and upon this were first-cousins. I don't know why I felt this; I only record it for you without comment.

'So she stood there talking, a hard devil behind all her commonplace words. I hated her; I wished myself dead. My

135

one consolation, that Westmacott did not know what a fool he was making of me, was gone, since Ruth was making of me a much bigger fool, and was doing it in all consciousness. How I hated her! and at the same time, through her hatefulness, she seemed to me more than ever desirable. Westmacott knew nothing of what had gone before, but, sensitive as he was underneath his brutality, with the unmistakable sensitiveness of the Latin, he was, I think, aware of some atmospheric presence in the room. At any rate, he realised the devilish attraction of his wife, and in his spontaneous foreign way he put out his hand to touch hers. An English farmer! I nearly laughed again. When he did this, she sat down on the arm of his chair, and, putting her arms round his neck, laid her cheek against his hair, with her eyes on me all the while. Then, as though she had released some lever by her action, he turned within her arms, and kissed her savagely.

'The next thing I knew was that I was walking at an extraordinary pace across the fields, gasping in the air, and that strong shudders like the shudders of a fever were running down my frame. I am not really very clear as to how I spent the rest of that day, or of the days that followed. Do you know that familiar nightmare in which you roll a tiny ball no bigger than a cartridge-shot between your finger and thumb, till it grows and grows into an immense ball that overwhelms you? So through a nightmare haze I rolled the memory of that horrible little scene into a tight ball, till I could see neither beyond nor above it, but all my horizon was obscured by the distended pellet in my brain. And during all this time I moved about the world like a man in full possession of his senses, making my dispositions for a long absence abroad, talking to my banker out of the depths of a leather arm-chair, buying my tickets from Thomas Cook, directing the packing of my luggage, and, so far as I know, neither my banker nor Cook's clerk nor the club

136

servant realised that anything was amiss with me.

'I had only one desire: to get away, to think. I was as impatient for solitude as the thirsty man is for water. I resented every one in my surroundings and my delay in London much as I had resented Westmacott and my delay in the kitchen. Until I could get away, I banished all thought from my mind; only, as I tell you, the scene in the kitchen remained whirling and whirling beyond my control.

'Finally I escaped from England, and as I lay sleepless, buffeted all night in the train, one thought persisted like music in my brain, "To-morrow I shall be alone, I shall be rid of nightmare, I shall be able to dwell luxuriously upon the magical moment, and all that it means, all that it entails. Yes! I shall be alone with it, for weeks, months, years if I like. I shall no longer be forced to grant undue proportion to the nightmare; until now it has made black night of my days, but to-morrow it will recede like a fog before the sun, and I shall dwell in the crystal light of the mountain-tops."

'My destination was – I wonder if you have guessed it already? – Sampiero. I knew that there I was certain of peace, hospitality, familiar rooms. Besides, it was there that I had spoken to you for so many hours of the opening chapters of this story, and I had a fancy that if I took my dreamings up to the clump of pines, the shadows of those earlier chapters might come, re-evoked to brush like soft birds against my cheek. I had planned to go up to the clump of pines on my first evening after dinner. My dear fellow, do not be offended when I tell you that as I arrived by that absurd mountain railway at Sampiero. I was seized by a sudden panic that some desire for rest and peace might have brought you, like myself, to the same old haunt. I suppose that I was in an excitable state of mind already, for by the time I reached our old lodging-house I was in a fever and a passion of certainty that I should find you there before me. Signora Tagliagambe was at the door to welcome me, but I

137

rushed at her with inquiries as to whether I was or was not her only guest. She stared at me with obvious concern for my reason. There were no other guests. I had my former room, also the sitting room to myself. I should be completely undisturbed.

'I recovered myself then, realising that I had been a fool, as I dare say you are thinking me at this moment. A delicious peace came stealing over me, the peace of things suspended. I was half tempted to give myself the luxury of putting off my first visit to the stone-pines until the following day. But the evening fell in such perfection that I wandered out, much as you and I have often wandered out to sit there in silence, sucking at our pipes; in the days, I mean, before I asked you that memorable question about the Weald of Kent.

'So there I was, at length, at peace, and I stretched myself out on the ground beneath the pines, pulling idly at a tuft of wild thyme, and rubbing it between my hands till the whole evening was filled with its curious aromatic scent, that came at me in gusts like a tropical evening comes at one in gusts of warmth. I had not yet begun to think, for, knowing that the moment when thought first consciously began to well up in my spirit would take its place in the perspective of my life not far short of that other moment on whose sacredness I scarcely dared to dwell, I put it off, even now, when it had become inevitable, torturing myself with the Epicureanism of my refinement. I was thirsty, thirsty, thirsty, and though the water stood there, sparkling and clear, I still refused myself the comfort of stretching out my hand.

'And then it came. Slowly and from afar, almost like pain running obscurely and exquisitely down my limbs, reflection returned to me like light out of darkness. I lay there absolutely motionless, while in my head music began to play, and I was transported to palaces where the fountains rose in jets of living water. Light crept all round me, and music, music . . . a great chorus, now, singing in unison;

swelling and bursting music, swelling and bursting light, louder and louder, brighter and more dazzling; a deafening crash of music, a blinding vision of light.

'I stood at last on the sunlit peak.

'All around me, but infinitely below, stretched the valleys and plains of darkness where I had dragged out my interminable days. I looked down upon them from my height, knowing that I should never return. I knew that I now stood aloft, at liberty to examine the truth which had come to me, turning it over and over in my hands like a jewel, playing with it, luxuriating in its possession. It was to be mine, to take at will from the casket of my mind, or to return there when other, prosaic matters claimed my attention. But, whether I left it or whether I took it out, I should bear it with me to the ends of the earth, and death alone could wrench me from its contemplation.

'What a lunatic you must think me after this rhapsody! What! you will say, does the man really mean that he wouldn't exchange the recollection of a moment for the living, material presence of the woman concerned? Well, it is very natural that you should think me a lunatic, but have patience; take into consideration my life, which has been lived, as you know, alone; always in unusual places, with no one near my heart. Living, material presences come to have comparatively little significance after twenty or thirty years of solitude. Try it, and you will see. One drifts into a more visionary world, peopled by shadowy and ideal forms; memories assume incredible proportions and acquire an unbelievable value; one browses off them like a camel off his hump. Do you begin to understand now that this great, shining, resplendent moment should rush in to fill a mind so dependent on the life unreal? One must have something, you see, and if one can't have human love one must fall back upon imagination. Hence the romantic souls of spinsters. . . .

'And hence, I might say, a great many other things which practical men barely acknowledge. I find myself straying off down paths of thought which may lead me into swamps of digression. Hence religion, hence poetry, hence art, hence love itself – the spiritual side of love. All these things, unpractical, inconvenient, unimportant things, all sprung from a craving in man's nature! A craving for what? Hasn't he been given strength, health, bodily well-being, hunger and thirst, fellowmen to fight, and fists to fight them with? What more does the creature want? He wants a thing called Beauty, but what it is he can't tell you, and what he wants to do with it when he's got it he can't tell you; but he wants it. Something that he calls his soul wants it. A desire to worship . . . Beauty, a purely arbitrary thing. All men strive after it, some men so little that they are themselves unconscious of the desire, other men so passionately that they give up their whole lives to its pursuit; and all the graded differences come in between.

'Here am I, then, a man of irregular and spasmodic occupation, an unsatisfactory, useless member of society, I'll admit, useless, but quite harmless; an educated man, what you would call an intellectual, not endowed with a brain of the good, sound type, but with a rambling, untidy sort of brain that is a curse to himself and a blessing to nobody. Here am I, without one responsibility in the world, with nothing to do unless I go out and forage for it, living alone with books, dabbling in this and that, and necessarily thrown for a certain number of hours each day on my own resources. You cannot wonder that my life of the imagination – as I will call it – becomes of supreme importance to me as my only companion. It had been a singularly blank life, so blank that when I went out for walks alone I used to fall back on repeating verse aloud, so you see it was a life of books, and man wants more than that. He wants something

140

that shall be at once ideal and personal. There is only one thing which fulfils those two conditions: Woman. But, you will say, if there's no woman in a man's life he has only himself to blame. You're right; I don't know why I never set out to find myself a woman, perhaps because I was too hard to please, perhaps because I knew myself to be too fickle and restless. You used to laugh at me when I said this. Of course, I don't pretend that there haven't been incidents in my life; but they never lasted, never satisfied me for long; they weren't even good to think about afterwards. Anyway, there I was: free, but lonely.

'And now I had got this new, precious, incredible thing to think over. I am afraid to tell you how long I stayed at Sampiero, doing nothing, lapped in my thoughts as in a bath of warm water. My conversation with Ruth had been brief, and I knew every word of it by heart; my hour started from when I had come up to her house and had stolen surreptitiously to the doorway to take her unawares, and had stood there with a smile on my lips, waiting for her to look up. I saw again the light and the flowers and the baby in the cradle. I felt again the swimming in my head as I looked, for the first time, it seemed, into the beauty of her face. I heard again my own voice saying, "Ruth! Ruth! you must come with me."

'But I told you all that before; why do I repeat it? Because I lived through it all an infinitude of times myself. I thought I couldn't exhaust the richness of my treasure. Nor could I, but after a while I found that my perfect contentment was being gradually replaced by a hunger for something more; I was human; the imagination wasn't enough.

'I began to want Ruth, Ruth herself, warm and living, and when I made this discovery I took a step I had long since prepared in my mind, foreseeing the day when dissatisfaction would overcome me: I left Sampiero and joined a party that was going into Central Africa after ivory.

III

'THE change in my existence was two-fold; I was now busy instead of idle, and in my thoughts I was unhappy instead of happy. At moments, indeed, I was so acutely unhappy that I welcomed desperately the preparations of our expedition which gave me plenty to do. I looked back to my months at Sampiero as one of the best periods of my life. One of my new companions asked me what I had been doing since the end of the war. I replied,—

' "I've been on a honeymoon with a thought," and he stared at me as though I were mad, and never quite trusted me for the rest of the expedition.

'I was busy before we started, and that took my mind off my own affairs, but on the ship I was again unoccupied; I used to lean my arms on the rail and stare down into the churning water, and feel my heart being eaten out as though by scores of rats with pointed teeth. I longed, I longed madly, for Ruth. In those days I used to think of her as a person, not as an abstraction; I wondered whether she was unhappy or fairly contented; I tried to draw up in my mind a scheme of her relations with Westmacott. But I couldn't; I couldn't face that just then, I put it off. I knew that sooner or later I must think the whole thing out, but when one has a score or more of years in front of one, one can afford to delay.

'Apart from this, I enjoyed my African experience; the men I was with were all good, dull fellows; I didn't make friends with any of them, beyond the comradeship of every day. What I enjoyed were the days of hunting, and the nights of waiting under such stars as I'd never seen; well, I suppose it is all lying there now as I write, just as I used to think of the untroubled Weald lying there spread under an English sky. It's funny to think of places you've been to, existing just the same when you aren't there. Yes, I liked Africa, and I tried to live in the present, but when the expedition was over, and I found myself landed alone at Naples, I realised with a shock that I had only succeeded in putting ten months of my life away behind me, and that an unknown quantity of years stretched out in front.

'I was sitting outside my hotel after luncheon, smoking, and looking over that most obvious and panoramic of bays. I hated Naples, I hated Italy; I thought it a blatant, superficial country, with no mystery, therefore no charm. I had almost made up my mind to take ship for Gibraltar, when a voice beside me said,—

' "You look pretty blue."

'I turned round and saw a long, leggy creature stretched out on a deck-chair beside me; he was squinting up at me from under a straw hat.

' "I feel it," I replied "about as blue as that sea."

' "What are you going to do?" he went on.

'I told him that I had just been thinking of going to Gibraltar.

' "And what'll you do when you get there?"

' "I hadn't thought of that," I answered.

' "On a holiday?" he inquired.

' "No," I said, "I don't work; I lead an aimless sort of life."

' "Great mistake," said he.

'I agreed.

' "How did it come about?" he asked.

'Somehow I found myself telling him.

' "When I was young – that is to say, after I had left Oxford – I thought I'd like to see the world, so I started; I travelled, stopping sometimes for six months or so if I liked the place. Then when I got tired of that, I took to

143

specialising in different subjects, giving a year, two years, three, to each. So I drifted on till the war, and here I am."

' "I see," he said. "And now you're bored."

' "Yes," I said, adding, "and worse."

'He made no comment on that; I don't know whether he heard. He said presently, in the same tone as he would have used to remark on current politics,—

' "I'm going to Ephesus to-morrow, you'd better come with me. My name's MacPherson."

' "All right," I said, "I'll come. My name's Malory. What are you going to do at Ephesus?"

'He replied, "Excavate."

'That will tell you what MacPherson was like: an eccentric, laconic sort of fellow; he never argued, he just made proposals, and, whether they were accepted or declined, nodded briefly in acquiescence without further discussion. For a long time I thought that I should never get any further with him, then gradually I began to find him out: a grim, sardonic soul, with only one passion in life, if I can give the name of passion to a determination so cold and unshakable; I mean his passion for excavation. I have seen him labouring for hours under the sun, dusty and indistinguishable from the ruins among which he worked, apparently tireless and thirstless; I have seen him labour like a man under the domination of a great inspiration, of a force such as drives fanatics to cut their own heads and cover their own backs with wales from the rod, but I have never heard an expression of delight or enthusiasm, or even of satisfaction, escape his lips at the result of his labours. Scientists and archæologists came to him with respect, invited his opinion, paid him compliments evidently sincere; he listened in total indifference, neither disclaiming nor acknowledging, only waiting for them to have done that he might get back to his work.

'Such was the man with whom I now lived, and you may imagine that I was often puzzled to know what had prompted his original invitation to me. I could, of course, have asked him, but I didn't. He took my presence absolutely as a matter of course, made use of me, — at times I had to work like a navvy, – never gave me his confidence, never expected mine. It was a queer association. We lived in a native house not far from the site of the temple on the hill above the ramshackle Turkish village of Ayasalouk, and one servant, an Albanian, did our housework for us, washed our clothes, and prepared our meals. We shared a sitting-room, but our bedrooms were separate; it was a four-roomed house. Occasionally, about once a month, MacPherson would go down into Smyrna and return next day with provisions, cigarettes, and a stock of tools and clothes, and sometimes an English paper.

'He let me off on Sundays, ungraciously, grudgingly, if silence can be grudging. I insisted upon it. At Pennistans' I had had a half-holiday on Sunday, and at Ephesus I would have it too. But here my hours of freedom were spent in loneliness. Lonely I would tramp off to the banks of the Cayster, and, standing among tall bulrushes and brilliant iris, would fish dreamily for mullet, till the kingfishers swept back, reassured, to the stream and joined me in my fishing.

> *Jam varias pelagi volucres, et quæ Asia*
> *circum*
> *Dulcibus in stagnis rimantur prata Caystri.*

You will admit, I think, that the quotation is singularly apposite. Or, as with Ruth, I had climbed the hills above the Weald, I would climb alone the heights of Mount Coressus, where the golden angelica surged about me, or the heights of Prion, which showed me, across the plain of Ephesus, the flatter plain of deep blue sea, broken by the summits of Samos – the very sea, the very Samos, where Polycrates flung forth his ring in defiance of the gods.

'A certain number of travellers came to Ephesus, whom MacPherson regarded with a patient disdain, but whom I welcomed as messengers of the outside world. I wanted to question them, but they were always so eager to question me, making me into a sort of guide, and inveigling me into doing them the honours of the place. This used to annoy MacPherson, though he never said anything; I think he felt it as a sort of desecration. I could see him watching me with disapproval, standing there among the columns in his dust-coloured shirt and trousers and sombrero hat, leaning his hands on the handle of his pick-axe, a hard, muscular man, thin and wiry as an Australian bush-settler. The tourists questioned me about him and about our life, but I noticed they rarely approached him, or, if they did so once, they did not do so twice. After talking to me, they would move away, decide – thankfully – among themselves that I could not be offered a tip, and finally would stroll off in the direction of our little house. Here I had dug a little garden in imitation of the Kentish cottages I knew so well; just a few narrow beds in front of the house, where I had collected the many wild flowers that grew on the neighbouring hills. MacPherson took an odd, unexpected interest in my garden. He brought me contributions, rare orchids and cyclamen which my eyes had missed, brought them to me gravely, carrying them cupped in his hands with as much tenderness as a child carries a nest full of eggs. He stood by me silently watching when I put them in with my trowel in the cool of the evening. Of course we got terribly burnt up in the summer, but in the spring my garden was always merry, and, if it added to my homesickness, it also helped to palliate it.

'MacPherson had evidently never thought of making the place less dreary than it naturally was; I have no great idea of comfort myself, but I can't live without flowers, and so

146

my instinct, which began in a garden, produced itself into other improvements; I bought a mongrel puppy off a shepherd, and its jolly little bark of welcome used to cheer our home-coming in the evening; then I made MacPherson bring back some chickens from Smyrna, a suggestion which seemed to horrify him, but to which he made no objection; finally I grew some flowers in pots and stood them in the windows. Oh, I won't disguise my real purpose from you: I was trying to make that rickety Turkish house as like a Kentish cottage as possible. I even paved a garden path – MacPherson examined every stone with the minutest care before I was allowed to lay it down – and finished it off with a swing-gate. Then it struck me that a swing-gate in mid-hillside looked merely absurd, so I contrived a square of wooden fencing all round our little property. Lastly, I hung a horse-shoe, which was a mule-shoe really, over the door.

'I tell you, the more the resemblance grew, the more and the less homesick I got. It was at once a pain and a consolation. There were times when I almost regretted my enterprise, and wanted to tear up the path, destroy the garden, strangle the puppy, and throw away the flowers, letting the whole place return to the bleakness from which I had rescued it. I wanted to do this, because my efforts had been too successful, and as a consequence I expected to see Ruth appear in that doorway, white sewing in her hands, and a smile of welcome to me – to me! – in her eyes. I have often come home pleasantly tired from my day's work, fully though sub-consciously confident that I should see her as I have described. . . .

'That garden of mine had many narrow escapes. But I kept it, and I went on with my pretence, perfecting it here and there: I got a kennel for the puppy, and I got some doves that hung in a wicker-cage beside the door. At last the counterfeit struck MacPherson.

' "Why," he said, stopping one evening, "it looks quite English."

' "Do you think so?" I replied.

' "Yes," he said, "but I tell you what, those flowers are wrong. An English cottage garden doesn't have orchids; it has mignonette. How can we get some mignonette?"

' "I might write home for some," I said slowly.

'It was true: I might write home for some. To whom? Mrs Pennistan would send it me. Then it would have a sentimental value which it would lack coming from a seedsman. But I knew quite well that it was not to Mrs Pennistan that I intended to write.

'After dinner I brought out a little folding table and set it by the door. MacPherson was there already, playing Patience as was his invariable habit.

' "Going to write letters?" he asked, seeing my inkpot.

' "Yes," I said, "I'm going to write for the mignonette."

'I headed my letter, "Ephesus," an address which always gave me satisfaction; not that I often had an opportunity of writing it.

' "MY DEAR RUTH,—I am writing to you from a hill-side in Turkey to ask you if you will send me some seeds of mignonette for my garden; it is very easy to grow, and I think would do well in this soil. You would laugh if you could see my house, it is not like anything you have ever seen before. Please send me the mignonette soon, and a line with it to tell me if you are well."

'I addressed it, "Mrs Rawdon Westmacott, Vale Farm, Weald, Kent, England," and there it lay on my table grinning and mocking at me, knowing that it would presently cross the threshold I was dying to cross, and be taken in the hands I was dying to hold again.

' "Done?" said MacPherson. "Where have you ordered the seeds from? Carter's?"

' "No," I said, "I've asked a friend for them," and some

148

odd impulse made me show him the address on the envelope.

'He read it, nodded, and said nothing. I was disappointed, though really I don't know what I should have answered had he questioned me.

'After that my days were filled with one constant thought. I calculated the nearest date, and then coaxed myself into the belief that there would be a delay after that date had come and gone; a long delay; perhaps a month. So many things might happen, Ruth might not be able to get the seed, she might put off writing, she might simply send the seed with no covering letter at all. This last thought was unendurable. It grew, too, in my mind: people of Ruth's upbringing and education didn't like writing letters, they didn't like perpetuating their opinions so irrevocably as ink on paper perpetuated them, and anyway they always had a conviction that the letter once written, would not arrive, especially at an unheard-of place like Ephesus. It was difficult enough to imagine the safe transit of a letter from one English county to another, but that a letter posted in the Weald of Kent should arrive in due course at a place out of the Bible was unthinkable. . . . I became daily more persuaded that she would not write, and daily my gloom deepened. MacPherson noticed it.

' "Feel ill?" he asked.

' "No, thanks," I said, annoyed.

' "You're not starting cholera?" he suggested suspiciously.

' "No, I tell you; I'm perfectly well."

' "Glad of that," he said, but I told myself peevishly that his gladness was based entirely on considerations of his own convenience.

'Ten days passed; a fortnight; three weeks; I was in despair. Then one morning, as I came out of our door with a basket in my hand to pick up a couple of eggs for breakfast, I saw a large magenta patch down below, on the hilly pathway which led from our house to the village. This, I knew, must be the old negro woman who brought our rare letters. I watched her; the morning was slightly misty, for it was very early, not long after sunrise, and I saw her black face emerge from the plum-coloured mashlak she wore. I started off to meet her. She came toiling up the hill, panting and blowing, for she was enormously fat, but an indestructibly good-humoured grin parted her lips over her gleaming teeth, and suddenly I fancied a grotesque resemblance to Mrs Pennistan, and I laughed aloud as though a good omen had come to speed me.

'I came up to her. Her black skin was glistening with moisture, and her vast body rocked and swayed about inside her gaudy magenta wrapper; I suspected it of being her only covering. Still, I almost loved her as with a chatter of Turkish she produced a great black arm and hand out of the folds of her mashlak – a fat black hand so ludicrously like Mrs Pennistan's fat white one, holding a little packet which she tendered to me.

'I summoned my Turkish to thank her; this called forth a deluge of conversation on her part, with much shining of teeth and clattering of bangles, but I shook my head regretfully, and she, heaving her huge shoulders and displaying her palms in equivalent regret, turned herself round and started on the easier downward road to Ayasalouk. Could Ruth but have seen this voluminous magenta emissary! for the packet I held was indeed from Ruth and bore the Weald postmark.

'I sat down by the roadside to open it. The seeds were there, and a letter, written in a round, Board-school hand, accompanied them. I was suddenly unable to read; it was the first word, remember, that had come to me from her since that memorable day. I was more than moved; I was shaken, like a tree in the wind.

'I read:

' "Vale Farm, Weald,
' "15 IV. 22.

' "DEAR MR MALORY – Yours to hand, and enclosed please find mignonette seeds as requested. I hope they will do well in your garden. Our garden was baked hard in the drowt last summer, but hope we will have more favourable weather this year. My husband and the boys are well, and send their respects. Well, must stop now as have no more news. Hoping this finds you well, I am,

' "Yours obediently,
' "R. WESTMACOTT."

'That was her letter – I have it here to copy, old and worn and torn – and in its stiff conventionality, its pathetically absurd phraseology, it seemed to tear my heart into little fluttering ribbons. Anything less like her I couldn't conceive, yet she was indescribably revived to me; I saw her bending, square-elbowed, over that bit of paper, hesitating when she came to the word "drought," deciding wrong, tipping up the octagonal, penny bottle of ink which hadn't much ink left in it; I saw her getting the seeds, making up the parcel, copying "Ephesus" conscientiously from my letter. You may think me sentimental; it was the only tangible thing I had of hers.

'MacPherson met me at the top of the path.

' "Letters?" he said.

' 'Not for you, but I've got the mignonette seed."

'He looked puzzled.

' "The what?" Heavens! the man had forgotten! "Oh, yes, I remember," he said; "let's go and put it in."

'I had got ready a prepared seed-bed, where I think I had broken up every lump of earth, however insignificant, with my own fingers, and here I sowed Ruth's packet of seed. I sowed it with the solemnity of a priest sacrificing at the altar. MacPherson looked on as was his wont, unaware of anything special in the occasion, and rather impatient to get to breakfast.

'In a few weeks' time the plants began to show; I watered them, and cherished them, thinned them out, put wire round them, treated them as never was hardy annual treated before. Soon the fragrant thing was all round our doorstep. I felt like a prisoner tending the plant between the flag-stones of his prison, or like Isabella with her pot of Basil. I laughed at myself, but still I continued my cult, and the nightly watering of the flowers throughout the hot summer became to me a species of ritual.

'You used to call me a pagan; that's as it may be, but any-way I dedicated my whole garden to Ruth, growing my flowers in her honour, enlarging my plot, planting the hill-side outside the fence with broom and wild things, till the whole place was rich and blooming. This labour gave me the greatest satisfaction. My dreadful hungry craving for her living presence was momentarily lulled and I returned to that happier frame of mind when, as I described to you, I was content to live in the imagination. I could set her up now as a kind of idealised vision of all that was beautiful, all that was desirable. She was the deity of my garden, almost the deity of the great temple where I laboured. I should think MacPherson would have half killed me had I hinted this to him.

'I was happy again, and in the next spring I got Ruth to send me out some more seeds from her own garden. With them came another stilted little note, but this time there was a postscript: was I ever coming back to England? That dis-turbed me terribly; I knew it contained no double meaning, for I knew perfectly well that Ruth would never leave her children to come away with me, but at the same time it stirred up my sleeping desire to see England again. I analysed this, and found that I didn't in the least want to see

England; I only wanted to see Ruth. This frightened and distressed me; I had been so calm, so comparatively happy, and here a few idle words had thrown me into a state of emotional confusion. The ruins seemed odious to me that day, my garden seemed a mockery, and in the evening I said to MacPherson,—

' "I am afraid I must go away."

'He said, "Oh?' less in a tone of dismay than of polite inquiry, and, as usual, of acceptance.

' "I am getting restless here," I said, "but if I go and stretch my limbs a bit I shall be better; I will come back."

' "All right," he answered, as though there were no more to be said on the matter.

' "That is, if you want me," I added, provoked.

' "Naturally I shall be glad to see you whenever you choose to come back," he said, without a trace of emotion or cordiality in his tone.

IV

BEFORE I left I made arrangements with the Albanian to look after my garden during my absence; much as I hated leaving it to other hands I felt that I must get away or I should begin to scream upon the hills of Ephesus. I went down to Smyrna without much idea of what I should do after that, but when I got there I found a ship bound for Baku, so, thinking I might as well go there as anywhere else, I got on board and we sailed that night. I don't want to give you a tedious account of my journey; I will only tell you that it did me all the good in the world, and that I walked up to Ephesus one evening in the late autumn with my toothbrush in my pocket and real home-coming excitement in my heart. There was the little house; there was my garden, showing quite a fair amount of colour for the time of year; there was MacPherson sitting outside, gravely playing his interminable Patience. The puppy – puppy no longer, but a dog of almost inconceivable ugliness – rushed out barking, and seized the ankle of my trousers in its joy. MacPherson looked up.

‘ "Hallo," he said. "Evening."

‘ "Evening," I replied, and sat down.

‘ "I believe this Patience is coming out," he said presently.

‘ "Is it?" I answered, vastly amused.

‘ "Yes," said MacPherson, "if I could only get the three I should do it. Ah!" and he made a little pounce, and shifted some cards. "Done it," he announced in a tone of mild triumph, adding regretfully, "now it won't come out again for at least a week."

‘ "That's a pity," I said.

' "Yes," he replied, "I reckon it comes out about once in every hundred times. Garden's all right, isn't it?"

' "Splendid," I said; "I was just looking at it. How's your digging?"

' "That's all right, too. Glad you're back."

'I was surprised at this and gratified, but my gratification was damped when his obvious train of thought had occurred to me.

' "Ready to work to-morrow?" he asked, confirming my suspicion.

' "Rather."

' "That's all right," he said again.

'He did not ask me where I had been, and I thought I would not volunteer it, but after a day or two I did.

' "I went to the Caucasus," I said.

'He answered, "Oh." I was not offended, only greatly amused; he was a perpetual joy to me, that man.

'I took up my life again very much where I had left it, and now again a change came about in my thoughts; they were constantly occupied with Ruth and with that examination I had so long put off, of her relations with her husband. As the story which I shall presently tell you will make them quite clear to you – if anything so involved can ever be made quite clear – I shall not bore you now with my own conjectures. It is quite bad enough that I should bore you with my own life, but you will agree that I couldn't say to you. "Now ten years passed," without giving you the slightest idea of my movements during those ten years. Those ten years, you see, are my little Odyssey; I look back on them now, and I see them in that light, but while they lasted I naturally didn't look on them as a poetic spell out of my life; no, I looked on them as a sample of what my life would be till it came to the simplest of all ends: death. I supposed that I should stay at Ephesus with MacPherson till he got tired of excavating, which I knew would never happen, or till I got tired of excavating, which I thought was much more likely, or till the authorities turned us out. After that I didn't know what I should do, but I thought, so far as I ever thought about it at all, that something would turn up in much the same way as the boat at Smyrna had turned up to take me to Baku. What did occasionally exercise my mind was the question whether I should ever see England again? If I couldn't have Ruth I didn't want to go to England; it would be a torment to know her so near; but on the other hand I foresaw that as an old man of seventy I should not want to be still knocking about the world or excavating at Ephesus. The ravens would have to provide. Why make plans? Fate only steps in and upsets them. How angry I used to make you by talking about Fate, do you remember?

'Meanwhile my Odyssey continued, and I found that every year my restlessness returned to me, so that sooner or later the moment always came when I said to MacPherson,—

' "I am afraid I shall have to go away to-morrow," and he replied invariably,—

' "Oh? All right."

'I went to all manner of places, but never to England, and always in the autumn I returned to Ephesus to find Mac-Pherson there unchanged, always glad to see me because of my help in his work, and in all those years he never once asked me where I had been to. I forget now myself where I went, except that I never once went anywhere near England, much as I wanted to go, because I knew the temptation would be too strong for me. This journey of mine became thus an annual institution. There was another annual institution of which MacPherson knew only the outer and less important part; this was the arrival of seeds from England, with Ruth's little letter attached; I came to know all her phrases, which revolved with the years in a cycle: she hoped the seeds would do well with me; her garden had been dried up, or washed out, as the case might be, the previous summer –

there is never a perfect summer for a gardener, just as there is never a perfect day for a fisherman; her children were well and sent their respects, varied by love; her husband was well too; she must stop as she had no more news, or as the post was going. Occasionally she ended up, "In great haste," though what the haste could be in that leisurely life I failed to imagine.

'I came to look for this letter in my year as the devout man looks for a feast-day; it was, so to speak, my Easter. My little packet grew, that much-travelled little packet, which went with me on all my pilgrimages. I wondered whether she cherished my letters, over in England, as I cherished hers at Ephesus? In the meantime she was there, in the house I knew, living through these years in a calm monotony which was a consolation to me, because I could so well imagine it; I could call up a picture of her, in fact, at practically any moment of the day, for what variation could there be to her quotidian round of cooking, housework, washing, sewing? This was, I say, a pleasant reflection to me, though I was enraged to think that her care and labour should be expended upon another man and another man's children. A placid existence, broken only by the calving of cows, the farrowing of swine, the gathering in of crops. . . . And I at Ephesus!

'MacPherson never spared me my share of the work, and a hard taskmaster he was, as hard to himself as to me. In the summer we breakfasted soon after the dawn had begun to creep into the sky, then with pick and mattock we trudged to the ruins, there to toil until the heat of the sun glaring upon the quantities of white marble which lay about us drove us indoors until evening. MacPherson was always very grudging and resentful with regard to this enforced siesta. In fact he would not admit it as a siesta, but affected to consider it merely as a variation of work, and would remain below in our little sitting-room, turning over for the thousandth time his scraps and fragments of glass, pottery, and other rubbish, while I lay on my bed upstairs damning the mosquitoes and trying to go to sleep. No sooner had I dozed off than I would be aroused by MacPherson's remorseless voice calling up to know if I was ready. Evening in the ruins I did not mind so much; a little breeze often sprang up from the sea, and I had the prospect of an hour's gardening immediately in front of me. On the whole I was happy in those hours of toil. Living in my thoughts, and sparing just the bare requisite of consciousness to the needs of my tools, I became almost as taciturn as my companion. Yet I never came to look on Ephesus as a home; I was only a bird of passage – a passage lasting ten years, it is true, but still only a passage. I didn't see how it was going to end, but my old friend Fate stepped in at last and settled that for me.

'It was July, and my annual restlessness had been creeping over me for some time; besides, it was getting unpleasantly hot at Ephesus, and I panted for the cold air of the mountains. So I said to MacPherson at breakfast,—

' "I think the time for my yearly flitting has come round again; in fact, I think I'll be off to-day."

'I waited for the, "Oh? All right," but it didn't come. Instead of that, he said after a little pause,—

' "I wonder if you would put off going until to-morrow?"

'It was the first time I had ever heard him raise an objection to any suggestion of mine, and I was faintly surprised, but I said,—

' "Of course I will. One day's just as good as another. Got a special job for me?"

' "No," he said, "it isn't that."

'I did not question him; I had long since followed his lead, and we never questioned one another.

'Still, I wondered to myself, as one cannot help wondering when anything unusual, however slight, occurs to break

158

a regularity such as ours. A stone thrown in a rough sea falls unperceived, but thrown into a pond of mirror-like surface it creates a real disturbance. So all the morning I observed MacPherson as closely as I dared; I saw him go to get his things, and I detected a slight weariness in his walk; still he said nothing. It was glaringly hot at the ruins. I thought of suggesting that we should go home earlier than usual, and, turning round to look for MacPherson, I saw him at a little distance, sitting on a boulder, with his head in his hands. This was so unusual that I immediately crossed over to him.

' "I say, aren't you feeling well?"

'He raised to me a livid face.

' "I shall be all right presently. . . . A touch of the sun."

' "You must come indoors at once," I said firmly. "You must be mad to sit here in this heat. Can you walk?"

He rose with infinite weariness, but without a word of complaint, and attempted to lift his pick.

' "I'll take that," I said, taking it from him, and he gave it up without a word. "Is there anything else to bring?"

'He shook his head, and began to stumble off in the direction of the house. Long before we had reached home, I knew what was the matter with my companion. The sun was not responsible. He was in the grip of cholera.

'The Albanian, who was splashing cold water from a bucket over the tiled floor of our little sitting-room when we arrived, stared at us in astonishment. MacPherson, his face faded to the colour of wood-ashes, had his arm round my neck for support, and already the terrible cramps of the disease were beginning to twist his body as he dragged one leaden foot after the other. I called to Marco, and between us we half carried him upstairs and laid him on his bed, where he lay, silent, but drawing his breath in with the long gasps of pain, and with his arm flung across his eyes so that we should not observe his face.

'I drew Marco out on to the landing. I bade him saddle the mule and ride straight to the station, where he must take the train for Smyrna and return without delay with the English doctor. I did not think, in my private mind, that the doctor could arrive in time, or that he could do more than I could, who had some experience of cholera, but still I was bound to send for him. Marco nodded violently all the time I was speaking. I knew I could trust him; he was an honest man. I went back to MacPherson.

'I had never been into his bedroom before. The Venetian blinds were lowered outside the windows, and the floor and walls were barred with the resulting stripes of shade and sun. A plaid rug lay neatly folded across the foot of the bed. On the dressing-table were two wooden hair-brushes and a comb, on the wash-stand were sponges, but no possessions of a more personal nature could I discover anywhere. The man, it seemed, had no personal life at all.

'He was lying where I had left him, still breathing heavily; his skin was icy cold, so I covered him over with the quilt from my own room, knowing that it was no use attempting to get him into bed, and feeling, in a sympathetic way, that he would prefer to be left alone. I went to get what remedies I could from our medicine-chest downstairs, and as I was doing this my eye fell on his little cupboard where behind glass doors he kept his precious shards, all labelled and docketed in his inhumanly neat handwriting, and I wondered whether, in a week or so, I should see him sitting down there, fingering his treasures with hands that, always thin, would surely be shrunken then to the claws of a skeleton.

'It's bad enough to see any man in extreme agonies of pain, but when the man is an uncommunicative, efficient, self-reliant creature like MacPherson it becomes ten times worse. I felt that a devil had deliberately set himself to tear the seals from that sternly repressed personality. MacPherson, who had always assumed a mask to disguise any human feelings he may have had, was here forced, driven, tortured into the revelation of ordinary mortal weakness. I believe that, even through the suffering which robs most men of all vestiges of their self-respect, he felt himself to be bitterly humiliated. I believe that he would almost have preferred to fight his disease alone in the wilderness. Yet I could not leave him. He was crying constantly for water, which I provided, and besides this there were many services to render, details of which I will spare you. I sat by the window with my back turned to him whenever he did not need me, glad to spare him what observation I could, and glad also, I confess, to spare myself the sight of that blue, shrivelled face, tormented eyes, and of the long form that knotted and bent itself in contortions like the man-snake of a circus. . . . His courage was marvellous. He resolutely stifled the cries which rose to his throat, hiding his face and holding his indrawn breath until the spasm had passed.

'I knew that this stage of the disease would probably continue for two or three hours, when the man would collapse, and when the pain might or might not be relieved. The sun was high in the heavens when I noticed the first signs of exhaustion. MacPherson sank rapidly, and the deadly cold for which I was watching overcame him; I covered him with blankets – this he feebly resisted – and banked him round with hot water bottles, of which we always kept a supply in case of emergency. It was now midday, and I had continually to wipe the sweat from my face, but I could not succeed in bringing much warmth to poor MacPherson. He lay quiet and silent now, save when the fearful sickness returned, as it did at short intervals. I sat beside him, ready with the water for which he was continually asking.

'He was, as I have said, always thin, but by this time his face was cavernous; I could have hidden my knuckles in

161

the depression over his temples, and my fist in the hollow under his cheek-bones. His scant, reddish hair, always carefully smoothed, lay about his forehead in tragic wisps. His pale blue eyes showed as two smears of colour in their great sockets. His interminable legs and arms stirred at unexpected distances under the pile of blankets. He was very weak. I feared that he would not pull through.

'When the merciless sun was beginning to disappear round the corner of the house, MacPherson, who had been lying for the last hour or so in a state of coma, spoke to me in a low voice. I was staring in a melancholy way from my chair by his side, across the bed, between a chink of the Venetian blind; I don't know what I was thinking of, probably my mind was a blank. I started when I heard him whisper my name, and bent towards him. He whispered,—

' "I don't think I'm going to recover."

'Neither did I, and seeing that he had made the remark as a statement of fact, in his usual tone, though low-pitched, I waited for what he should say next. He said,—

' "I am sorry to be a bore."

'This was a hard remark to answer, but I murmured something. He went on, still in that hoarse whisper,—

' "I must talk to you first."

'I saw that he was perfectly lucid in his mind, and thinking that he wanted to give me some necessary instructions I encouraged him to go on, but he only shook his head, and I saw that he had fallen back into the characteristic apathy. I sat on, expecting the arrival of Marco and the doctor at any moment.

'Towards night, MacPherson roused himself again. He was so much weaker that I could barely make out the words he breathed.

' "It is time you went to water your garden."

'I shook my head. A distressed look came over his face, and to comfort him I said,—

' "Marco has promised to do it for me."

'He was content with that, and lay quiet with his long, long arms and thin hands outside the coverlet. I thought that he wanted to speak again, but had not the energy to begin, so, to help him, I suggested,—

' "Was there anything you wanted to say to me?"

'He nodded, more with his eyelids than with his head, then, bracing himself with pain for the effort, he whispered,—

' "You won't stay on here?"

'I answered, "No," feeling that to adopt a reassuring, hearty attitude would be an insult to the man.

'After a long pause he said,—

' "I want to be buried up here. By the ruins. I don't care about consecrated ground."

'An appalling attack of sickness interrupted him, after which he lay in such complete exhaustion that I thought he would never speak again. But after about half an hour, he resumed,—

' "Give me your word of honour. They will try to prevent you."

'I swore it – poor devil.

' "Bury me deep," he said with a grim, twisted smile, "or some one will excavate me."

'He seemed a little stronger, but I knew the recovery could only be fictitious. Then he went on,—

' "Will you do something else for me?"

' "Of course I will," I answered, "anything you ask."

' "My wife . . ." he murmured.

' "Your *wife*?" I said.

' "She's in London," he whispered, and he gave me the address, dragging it up out of the depths of his memory.

'In London! Even in that dim room, with the dying man there beneath my hand, I felt my heart bound with a physical sensation.

' "Just tell her," he added; "she won't mind. She won't make you a scene."

'He was silent then, but drank a great draught of water.

' "Is there any one else?" I asked.

'His head moved very feebly in the negative on the pillow.

' "And what am I to do with your things?" I asked lastly.

' "Look through them," he breathed; "nothing private. Give the fragments to the British Museum. I've made a will about money."

' "And your personal things? Would you like me to give them to your wife?"

' "Oh, no," he said wearily, " 'tisn't worth while." Then after a long pause in which he seemed to be meditating, he said, with evidently unconscious pathos, "I don't know. . . . Better throw them away."

'MacPherson died that night about an hour before the doctor came; Marco and the doctor had missed each other, and missed the trains, but the doctor reassured me that I had done all that was possible, and that had he arrived by midday he could not have saved MacPherson's life.

' "I suppose you will want to bring him down to the English cemetery at Smyrna?" he said, with an offer of help tripping on the heels of his remark. He looked horrified when I told him of MacPherson's wish and of my intention of carrying it out.

' "But no priest, I am afraid, will consent to read the burial service over him under those conditions," he said primly.

' "Then I will read it myself," I replied in a firm voice.

' "You must please yourself about that," said the doctor, giving it up. His attitude towards me, which had started by being sympathetic, was now changing subtly to a slight impatience. He took out his watch. "I am afraid I ought to be going," he remarked, "if I am to catch the last train down to Smyrna, and there seems to be nothing more I can do for you here. There will have to be a certificate of death, of course; I will send you that. And if you like I will stop in the village on the way, and send some one up to you; you understand me – a layer-out."

'I said that I should be much obliged to him, and, accompanying him as far as the front door, I watched him go with Marco and a lantern, the little parallelogram of yellow light criss-crossed with black lines, swaying to and fro in the night.

'I could not go to bed, and as I was anxious to leave

165

Ephesus as soon as possible, I thought I would employ my time in going through poor MacPherson's few possessions. As he said, there was nothing private. I sat downstairs in the sitting-room we had shared, with his tin box open on the table before me, shiny black, and the inside of the lid painted sky-blue. It was pitifully empty. His will was in a long envelope, a will making provision for his wife, and bequeathing the remainder of his income to an archæological society; there was also a codicil directing that his Ephesian fragments were to go, as he had told me, to the British Museum. The box also contained a diary, recording, not his life, but his discoveries; and a few letters from men of science. For the rest, there were his books, his clothes, his wrist-watch, his plaid rug, and a little loose cash in Turkish coins. And that was all. There was absolutely nothing else. Not a photograph, not a seal, not even a bunch of keys. Nothing private! I should think not, indeed.

'I sat there staring at the bleak little collection when Marco came in to say that he had returned with the layer-out. I went into the passage, and there I found our old negro post-woman, grinning as usual in her magenta wrapper; it seemed that she combined several village functions in her own person. I felt an instinctive horror at the thought of those black hands pawing poor MacPherson, but the thing was unavoidable, so I took her upstairs to where he lay in a repose that appeared to me enviable after the brief but terrible suffering he had undergone, and left her there, bending over him, the softer parts of her huge body quivering as usual under her mashlak. I went downstairs again, and stood outside to breathe the clean, cool air; the sky hung over me swarming with stars; I tried not to think of the old negress exercising her revolting profession on MacPherson's body.

'Next day two men in baggy trousers and red sashes came up to the house carrying the hastily-made coffin. Then we set

166

out, Marco, myself, and the two men with the coffin and MacPherson inside it. Providentially there were no tourists that day at Ephesus. Marco and I had been hard at work all the morning digging the grave, and as I drove my pick I reflected that this was, humanly speaking, the last time I should ever break up the flinty ground of Ephesus. After ten years! With regard to myself and my future, I dared not think; my present pre-occupation was to have finished with MacPherson and his widow.

'Well, I buried him up there, and may I be hanged if I don't think the man was better and more happily buried in the place he had loved, than stuck down in a corner of some unfriendly cemetery he had never seen. For myself – such is the egoism of our nature – I was thinking all the while that I would leave behind me a written request to be buried within sight of Westmacott's farm in Kent. And after I had buried him, and had got rid of Marco and the two men over a bottle of *raki* in the kitchen, I took all the flowers from my garden and put them on his grave, and I dug up some roots of orchid and cyclamen and planted them at his head and at his feet; but I don't suppose they ever survived the move, and probably to this day the tourists who wander far enough afield to stumble over the mound, say, "Why, some one has buried his dog out here."

'A week later I was in London, on a blazing August day which seemed strangely misty to me, accustomed as I was to the direct, unmitigated rays of the sun on the Ephesian hills. I still hadn't thought about my future, and I was resolved not to do so until, my interview with Mrs MacPherson over, I could look upon the whole of the last ten years as an episode of the past. I had tried to forget that I was in the same country as Ruth; but this had been difficult, for the train from Dover had carried me through the heart of Ruth's own county, a cruel, unforeseen prank of fortune;

167

I had pulled down the blinds of my railway carriage, greatly to the annoyance of my fellow-travellers, but these good people, who might have been involved with Fate in a conspiracy against me, had their unwitting revenge and defeated my object utterly by saying, as we flashed through a station, "That was Hildenborough; now we have to go through a long tunnel."

'Hildenborough! After ten years, during which I had consistently kept at least fifteen hundred miles between us, I was at last within two miles of her home. I nearly sprang out of the train at the thought. But I resolutely put it away, so resolutely that I found myself pushing with my hands and with all my force against the side of the railway carriage.

'It was too late, when I reached London, to do anything that day. I slept at my old club, where everybody started at the sight of me as of a ghost, and the following morning I went to the address MacPherson had given me. It was a block of flats, a long way up. I was left stranded upon the tiny landing by the lift-boy, who, with his lift, fell rapidly down through the floor as though pulled from below by a giant's hand. I rang the bell. It tinkled loudly; I heard voices within, and presently a woman came to open the door, with an expression of displeased inquiry on her face; a middle-aged woman, wearing a dingy yellow dressing-gown which she kept gathering together in her hand as though afraid that it would fall open.

' "Can I see Mrs MacPherson?" I asked.

'She stared at me.

' "There's no Mrs MacPherson here."

'I heard a man's voice from inside the flat,—

' "What is it, Belle?"

'She called back over her shoulder,—

' "Here's a party asking to see Mrs MacPherson."

' "Who is it?" asked the voice.

' "Who are you, anyway?" said Belle to me.

'"I have been sent here by Mr MacPherson, Mr Angus MacPherson, with a message for his wife," I said, "but as I have evidently made a mistake I had better apologise and go away."

'She looked suddenly thoughtful – or was it apprehensive?

'"No, don't go away," she said. "You haven't made a mistake. Come in."

'I went in, and she closed the door behind me. I followed her into the sitting-room where, amid surroundings at once pretentious and tawdry, a man, also in a dressing-gown, lay stretched on the sofa smoking cigarettes. He was handsome in a vulgar way, with black wavy hair and a curved, sensuous mouth.

'"Now," said Belle, "let's hear your news of Mr Angus MacPherson?"

'"First of all," I answered, "may I know who I am talking to?"

'Belle and the man exchanged glances.

'"Oh, well," she said then, "I am Mrs MacPherson all right enough. If you have really got a message for me, let's hear it."

'There was anxiety in her tone, and she edged nearer to the handsome man, and surreptitiously took possession of his hand.

'I did not think that the news of MacPherson's death was likely to cause much grief to his widow. I therefore said without preamble,—

'"I have come to tell you that he died a week ago of cholera. I was with him at the time, and I have brought you the certificate of his death, also his will. He left no other papers."

'"Angus dead?" said Angus's widow. "You don't say! Poor old Angus!"

'She was relieved by my words; I know she was relieved. She began reading the will with avidity. If I could find nothing else to admire about her, I could at least admire her candour.

'"He's left me five hundred a year," she said abruptly, "and the rest to some archi – what is it? society. Five hundred a year, and he had a thousand!"

'"Oh, come, Belle," said the handsome man, "that's better than nothing."

'She let her eyes dwell on his face with real affection, real kindliness.

'"Let's have a look at that will," he murmured lazily.

'She passed it across to him, sat down on a stool, clasped her knees, and became meditative.

'"Poor old Angus!" she repeated. "Fancy that! Well, he was rare fun in his day, wasn't he, Dick?"

'"No end of a dog," replied Dick without removing his eyes from the will.

'"Perhaps, if there are no questions you want to ask me, I had better be going now," I began. I was bewildered, for MacPherson, in spite of his eccentricities, had undoubtedly been a scholar and a man of refinement.

'Dick stirred from his spoilt torpor.

'"I suppose it is quite certain," he said, "that there is no mistake? I mean, it's quite certain he's dead?"

'"Quite," I answered rather grimly, as certain visions rose before my eyes. "I buried him myself"; and the flat with its dirty lace, its cheap pretension, melted away into the quiet beauty of Ephesus.

'I walked away from the building with an inexpressible loneliness at my heart, faced with my own immediate and remoter future, a problem I had hitherto refused to consider, but which now rushed at me like the oncoming wave rushes at the failing swimmer and overwhelms him. I had finished with Ephesus and MacPherson, and with Mac-Pherson's wife, and to say that I felt depressed would give you no idea of my feelings: an immense desolation took possession of me, an immense desolation, and more: an immense, soul-destroying disgust and weariness at the cruelty of things, a lassitude such as I had never conceived, so that I envied MacPherson lying for ever at peace, away from strife and difficulties and things that would not go right, among beautiful and untroubled hills, with wild flowers blooming round his grave. Yes, I envied him, I that am a sane man and have always prized rich life at its full value.

'And as I walked I met two men I had known, who spoke to me by name and stopped me.

' "Why, it's Malory," said one of them. "I haven't seen you lately. Somebody told me you had gone to Scotland?"

' "Yes," I said, "I went to Scotland."

'He asked me, "What part of Scotland?"

' "To Aberdeen," I cried, "to Aberdeen!" and laughed, and left them.

'I had been prepared to pass unrecognised after ten years, but for this friendliness, which had not "seen me lately," I was unprepared. I turned into a park, longing instinctively for the country as the only palliative for my loneliness and melancholy. In all London that day I think there was no lonelier soul than I. I would have sought you out, but in such a crisis of world-sorrow as was mine, I could desire only one presence – a presence I might not have. She could have annihilated my sorrow by a word, could have made me forget the dirt, and the irony; all that hurt me so profoundly – though I don't think myself a sentimentalist. For I was hurt as a raw sentimentalist is hurt, and this pain blended with my own trouble into a sea of despair. I wanted to find a haven of refuge, some beautiful gulf where the wind never blows, but where harmonious hills rise serenely from the water, and all is cultivated and easy and fertile.

'I sat for a long time under the trees, gazing immovably

171

at the ground between my feet, and then I got up mechanically, without any plan in my head, and wandered as mechanically home towards my club. My club burst incongruously enough on my dreams of a beautiful gulf; that, again, was part of the irony on this most cruel of days. But I had nowhere else to go to.

'I began to write to MacPherson's solicitors to inform them of their client's death; the new life was so empty that I clung for as long as I was able to the old. As I wrote, the hall-boy came and stood at my elbow.

' "Please, sir, there's a young woman asking to see you."

'A young woman? Could it be Belle? so equipped for the day's battle as to pass for young?

' "What's her name? what does she want?"

' "She won't say, sir; she wants to see you."

'I went out. Ruth was standing by the hall-door, plainly dressed in a dark coat and skirt, and a sailor hat, and holding a couple of faded red roses in her hand.

'I looked at her incredulously, and all the world stood still.

'She began, shyly and hurriedly,—

' "Oh, I don't want to bother you if you are busy . . ."

'That made me laugh.

' "I am not busy," I told her.

' "Oh, then perhaps I could speak to you for a few minutes? somewhere just quietly, and alone?"

'I glanced round. The porter was standing there with a face carved in stone.

' "You can't come in here," I said. "Where can I take you? Will you come to an hotel?"

' "Oh, no!" she said, shrinking, and I noticed her little gray cotton gloves.

' "At any rate, let us get away from here. Then we can think where to go."

'We went down the steps, crossed Piccadilly, and passed

into the Green Park. There I stopped, but she would not sit on the chair I suggested. She stood before me, her eyes downcast, and her gloved fingers twisting the stems of her roses. I bethought myself to ask her,—

' "How on earth did you find me, to-day of all days?"

' "I came to ask," she answered, still in that shy, hurried tone, "whether they knew when you would be coming to London."

' "And they told you I was there?"

' "Yes."

' "You came up from the Weald on purpose to ask that?"

' "Yes."

' "But why?"

'She was silent.

' "Why, Ruth?"

' "Because I wanted to see you."

' "To see me?"

' "To tell you something."

' "What is it?"

' "I can't tell you here," she murmured.

' "Come to an hotel," I said again, "we can get a private sitting-room; we can talk."

' "Oh, no, not that. I suppose . . . I suppose you wouldn't . . . I am sure you are busy."

' "No, no, on my honour, Ruth, I have absolutely nothing to do either to-day, or to-morrow, or the next day, or any day after that."

' "Sure?" she said eagerly, raising her eyes for one moment to mine and then lowering them again.

' "Quite sure."

' "Then," with sudden boldness, "will you come down to the Weald with me? now? at once?"

' "To the Weald? Of course I will, I'll do anything you like. We'll go straight to Charing Cross, shall we?"

173

' "Oh, yes, please, you are very good. And please, don't ask me any questions till we get there."

'My ten years' training with MacPherson proved invaluable to me now, and I can say with pride that neither by direct nor indirect means did I seek to extract any information from Ruth. Indeed, I was content to observe her as she sat by me in the cab, no longer the girl I remembered, but a woman of ripe beauty, and yet in her confused manner there was a remnant of girlishness, in her lowered eyes, and her tremulous lips. I saw that she sat there full of suppressed emotion, buoyed up by some intense determination which carried her over her shyness and confusion as a barque carries its passenger over high waves. I was too bewildered, too numb with joy, to wonder much at the cause of her journey.

'At Charing Cross she produced the return half of her third-class ticket from her little purse, refusing to let me pay the excess fare which would allow us to travel first. I think she was afraid of being shut alone with me into a first-class carriage, knowing that in the humbler compartment she could reckon on the security of company. So we sat on the hard wooden benches, opposite one another, rocking and swaying with the train, and trying to shrink away in our respective corners from the contact of the fruit-pickers who crowded us unpleasantly: Ruth sat staring out over the fields of Kent, her hands in their neat gray cotton gloves lying on her lap, and the tired roses drooping listlessly between her fingers; she looked a little pale, a little thin, but that subtle warmth of her personality was there as of old, whether it lay, as I never could decide, in the glow under her skin or in the tender curves of her features. She looked up to catch me gazing at her, and we both turned to the landscape to hide our confusion.

'Ah! I could look out over that flying landscape now with no need to pull down the window-blinds, and Penshurst station, when we reached it, was no longer a pang, but a rejoicing. The train stopped, I struggled with the door, we jumped out, the train curved away again on its journey, and we stood side by side alone on the platform.

'It was then about five o'clock of a perfect August day. Little white clouds stretched in a broken bank along the sky. Dorothy Perkins bloomed in masses on the palings of the wayside station. The railway seemed foreign to the country, the English country which lay there immovable, regardless of trains that hurried restless mankind to and fro, between London and the sea.

' "Let us go," I said to Ruth.

'We set out walking across the fields, infinitely green and tender to my eyes, accustomed to the brown stoniness of Ephesus. We walked in silence, but I, for one, walked happy in the present, and feeling the aridity of my being soaked and permeated with repose and beauty. Ruth took off her jacket, which I carried for her, walking cool and slender in a white muslin shirt. In this soft garment she looked eighteen, as I remembered her.

'We took the short cut to Westmacotts'. There it was, the lath and plaster house, the farm buildings, the double oast-house at the corner of the big black barn, simmering, hazy and mellow, in the summer evening. A farm-hand, carrying a great truss of hay on a pitchfork across his shoulder, touched his cap to Ruth as he passed. There was no sign of Westmacott.

' "Where . . ." I began, but changed my question. "Where are the children?"

' "I left them over with mother before I came away this morning," she answered.

'We went into the house, into the kitchen, the same kitchen, unchanged.

'She took refuge in practical matters.

175

'"Will you wait there while I take off my things and get the tea?"

'I sat down like a man in a dream while she disappeared upstairs. I was quite incapable of reflection, but dimly I recognised the difference between this clean, happy room of bright colours and shining brasses, and the tawdry, musty flat I had penetrated that morning, and the contrast spread itself like ointment over a wound.

'Ruth returned; she had taken off her hat and had covered her London clothes by a big blue linen apron with patch pockets. Her sleeves were rolled up to the elbow; I saw her smooth brown arm with the delicate wrist and shapely hand.

'"You'll want your tea," she said briskly.

'I had had nothing to eat since breakfast.

'You told me once in a letter that you had been to tea with Ruth, so you know the kind of meal she provides: bread, honey, scones, big cups, and tea in an enormous tea-pot. She laid two places only, moving about, severely practical, but still quivering with that suppressed excitement, still tense with that unfaltering determination.

'"It's ready," she said at length, summoning me.

'I couldn't eat, for the emotion of that meal alone with her was too strong for me. I sat absently stirring the sugar in my cup. She tried to coax me to eat, but her solicitude exasperated my over-strained nerves, and I got up abruptly.

'"It's no good," I said, "I must know. What is it, Ruth? What had you to tell me?"

'The moment had rushed at her unawares; she looked at me with frightened eyes; her determination, put to the test, hesitated.

'I went over to her and stood before her.

'"What is it, Ruth?" I said again. "You haven't brought me down here for nothing. Hadn't you better tell me before your husband comes in?"

'"He won't come in," she said, hanging her head so that

176

I could only see the wealth of her hair and her little figure in the big blue apron.

' "How do you know?" I asked.

' "He isn't here."

' "Where is he, then?"

'She raised her head and looked me full in the face, no longer frightened, but steady, resolute.

' "He has left me," she said.

' "Left you? What do you mean? For good?"

' "Yes. He's left me, the farm, and the children; he's never coming back."

' "But why? Good Heavens, why?"

' "He was afraid," she said in a low voice.

' "Afraid?"

' "Yes. Of me. Oh," she broke off, "sit down and I will tell you all about it."

VI

'AND then she unfolded to me the extraordinary story which, as I warned you at the very beginning of my letter, you will probably not believe. Nevertheless I offer it to you as a fact, so tangible a fact that it has driven a man – no chicken-hearted man – to abandon his home and source of wealth, his wife, and his children, and to fly without stopping to pack up his closest possessions, to America. I will not attempt to give you the story in Ruth's own words, because they came confusedly, transposing the order of events, dealing only with effects, ignoring the examination of causes. I will tell it you as I see it myself, after piecing together all my scraps of narrative and evidence. I only hope that, in dragging you away with me to Ephesus, and in giving you the events of my own life, you have not forgotten those who, in the Weald of Kent, are, after all, far more essential characters than I myself. Please try now to forget the Mac-Phersons, and project yourself, like a kind, accommodating audience, to the homestead, outwardly so peaceable, inwardly the stormy centre of so many complicated passions.

'And, again like a kind, accommodating audience, put ready at your elbow a little heap of your credulity, that you may draw on it from time to time, like a man taking a pinch of snuff.

'I do not know how far I should go back, perhaps even to the day when Ruth, in a wild state of reckless misery, ran away with Rawdon Westmacott. At once, you see, I am up against the question of their relationship, and you will understand that, situated as I now am with regard to Ruth, it isn't a question I like to dwell upon. There is a certain fellowship, however, between us, Ruth, Rawdon, and I, and when I consider that fellowship, my resentment – I will go further than that, and call it my loathing, my disgust – bends down like a springing stick and lies flat to the ground. By fellowship I mean, in myself, the restless spirit which drove me onward until, blinded by the habit of constant movement, I couldn't see the riches that lay close to my hand. In Ruth and Rawdon, I mean the passionate spirit that was the heritage of their common blood, and that drew them together even when she, by an accident of dislike, would have stood apart. We talk very glibly of love and indifference, but, believe me, it is largely, if it doesn't come by sudden revelation, a question of accident, of suggestion. It simply didn't occur to me that I might be in love with Ruth; I didn't examine the question. So I never knew. . . . And she, on her part, was there, young, southern, trembling on the brink of mysteries, pursued by Rawdon, whose character and mentality she disliked, from whom she, afraid, wanted to fly, and in whose arms she nevertheless felt convinced that she must end. From this I might have saved her. I see her now, a hunted creature, turning her despairing eyes on me, for a brief space seeking a refuge with Leslie Dymock, but finally trapped, captured, yielding – yielding herself to a storm of passion that something uncontrollable in her own nature rose up to meet.

'Seeing her in this light, I am overcome, not only with my stupidity and blindness, but with my guilt. Yet she was not altogether unhappy. It is true that Rawdon ill-treated and was unfaithful to her almost from the first, but it is also true that in their moments of reconciliation, which were as frequent as their estrangements, that is to say, very frequent indeed – in these moments of reconciliation she found consolation in the renewal of their curiously satisfying communion. I don't pretend to understand this. Ruth loved me – she has told me so, and I know, without argument, that she is speaking the truth – yet she found pleasure in the love of

179

another man, and even a certain grim pleasure in his ill-treatment of her. Or should I reverse my order, finding more marvel in her humility under his caresses than under his blows?

'What am I to believe? that she is cursed with a dual nature, the one coarse and unbridled, the other delicate, conventional, practical, motherly, refined? Have I hit the nail on the head? And is it, can it be, the result of the separate, antagonistic strains in her blood, the southern and the northern legacy? Did she love Westmacott with the one, and me with the other? I am afraid to pry deeper into this mystery, for who can tell what taint of his blood may not appear suddenly to stain the clear waters of his life?

'This, then, is Ruth, but in Westmacott the southern strain seems to be dominant; the clear English waters are tainted through and through. He is a creature of pure instinct, and when his instinct is aroused no logic, no reason will hold him, any more than a silk ribbon will hold a bucking horse. Ruth has told me of her life with him after he had gained possession of her, all his humility gone, changed into a domineering brutality; sometimes he would sit sulkily for hours, smoking and playing cards, and then would catch her to him and half strangle her with his kisses. She seems to have lived with him, the spirit crushed from her, meek and submissive to his will. I remembered the days when he used to lounge about Pennistans', leaning against the doorpost staring at her, and when she in disdain and contempt would clatter her milk-pans while singing at the top of her voice. Westmacott, I thought grimly, had had his own revenge.

'Once, as you know, she rebelled, but I do not think you know what drove her to it. Westmacott had brought another woman home to the farm, and had ordered his wife to draw cider for them both. When she refused, he struck her so that she staggered and fell in a corner of the room. She then collected her children and walked straight over to her father's house. How she tried to shoot Westmacott you know, for you were there. – I can't think about that story.

'But to come down to the day I went to the farm and asked her to come away with me. Westmacott suspected nothing at the time. About a week later he came home slightly drunk, and began to bully one of the children. Ruth cried out,—

' "Hands off my children, Rawdon!"

' "You can't stop me," he jeered.

'She said,—

' "I can. I nearly stopped you for ever once, and what's to prevent my doing it again?"

'He looked at her blankly, and his jaw dropped.

'For a week after that he was civil to her; their rôles were reversed, and she held the upper hand. Then he started shouting at her, but, brave in her previous success, she defied him,—

' "Stop swearing at me, Rawdon, or I'll go away and leave you."

'He roared with laughter.

' "Go away? Where to?"

'She says that she was wild, and did not care for the rashness of her words,—

' "I shall go to Mr Malory."

' "He wouldn't have you!" said Rawdon.

' "He would!" she cried. "He came here – you never knew – and tried to get me to go with him. And I'd have gone, but for the children. So there!"

'After this there was a pause; Rawdon was taken aback, Ruth was appalled by her indiscretion. Then Rawdon burst out into oaths, "which fouled the kitchen," said Ruth, "as though the lamp had been flaring." At this time, I suppose, I was at Sampiero.

'Of course, these and similar scenes could not go on perpetually. Their married life, although long in years, had been interrupted by over four years of war and absence, but now they found that they must settle down to life on a workable basis. They were married, therefore they must live together and make the best of it. Ruth tells me that they talked it out seriously together. A strange conversation! She undertook not to resent his infidelities if he, on his side, would undertake not to ill-treat her at home. So they sealed this compact, and in the course of time sank down, as the houses of the neighbourhood sank down into the clay, into a situation of no greater discontent than many of their prototypes.

'There was apparently no reason why this should not go on for ever. It did, indeed, let me tell you at once, go on for nearly ten years. They were quite tolerably happy; their children grew; their farm prospered; they were able to keep a servant. And then she saw a change coming over her husband.

'This is the thing which I do not expect you to believe.

'It began with his suggestion that Ruth should occupy the larger bedroom with the younger children, while he himself moved up to an attic at the top of the house, next to the boys' attic. She was astonished at this suggestion, and naturally asked him for his reasons. He could give none, except that it would be "more convenient." He shuffled uneasily as he said it. For the sake of peace, she agreed.

'But, suspicious now, she watched him closely, and he, realising that she was watching him, tried to writhe away from her vigilance. He would invent excuses to absent himself all day from the farm – a distant market, a local show – and would return late at night, creeping unheard up to his attic, there to slip off his clothes in the dark, or with the moonlight streaming in through his little latticed, dormer window. So for days he would contrive to meet his wife only at breakfast. His excuses were always convincing, and in them she could find no flaw. She might not have noticed his strange behaviour, but for the incident of the re-arranged bedrooms, and perhaps some feminine instinct which had stirred in her. She dared not question him, fearing a scene, but gradually she came to the not unnatural conclusion that he was keeping a second establishment where he spent most of his time.

'This left her indifferent; she had long since made her life independent of his, and the possible gossip of neighbours did not touch her as it would have touched a woman of commoner fibre. She had quite made up her mind that Rawdon spent all his nights away from home, returning shortly before she awoke in the morning. She did not resent this, especially as he had shown himself much gentler towards her of late. She was even vaguely sorry for him, that he should take so much trouble to conceal his movements. It must be very wet, walking through the long dewy grass of the fields so early in the morning.

'She was surprised to notice that his boots were never soaked through, as she logically expected to find them.

'One night she lay awake, thinking over all these things, when an impulse came to her, to go and look in his room. She got up quietly, slipping on her shoes and dressing gown, and stole out on to the landing. The house was dark and silent. She crept upstairs, and turned the handle of his door, confident that she would find the room empty. By the light of the moon, which poured down unimpeded by any curtain through the little oblong window in the sloping roof, she saw her husband's dark, beautiful head on the white pillow. He was sleeping profoundly. His clothes lay scattered about the floor, as he had thrown them off.

'So surprised was she – a surprise amounting, not to relief, but almost to dismay – that she stood gazing at him, holding the door open with her hand. Sensitive people and children will often wake under the influence of a prolonged gaze. Westmacott, who was a sensitive man beneath his brutality, and who further was living just then, I imagine, in a state of considerable nerve tension, woke abruptly with an involuntary cry as from a nightmare. He sat up in bed, flinging back the clothes – sat up, Ruth says, with staring eyes and the signs of terror stamped on all his features.

'"You! you!" he said wildly, "what do you want with me? in God's name what do you want?"

'She thought him still half-asleep, and replied in a soothing voice,—

'"It's all right, Rawdon; I don't want anything; I couldn't sleep, that's all; I'm going away now."

'But he continued to stare at her as though she had been an apparition, muttering incomprehensibly, and passing his hand with a wild gesture over his hair.

'"What's the matter, Rawdon?" she said, genuinely puzzled.

'At that he cried out,—

'"Oh, go away, leave me alone, for God's sake leave me alone!" and he began to sob hysterically, hiding his face in his sheets.

'Afraid that he would wake the children, she backed hastily out, shutting the door, and flying downstairs to her own room.

'He did not come to breakfast, but at midday he appeared, white and hollow-eyed, and climbed to his room, where he spent an hour screwing a bolt on to the inside of his door. When he came down again, he tried to slip furtively out of the house, but she stopped him in the passage.

'"Look here, Rawdon," she said, taking him by the shoulders, "what's the matter with you?"

'He shrank miserably under her touch.

'"There's nothing the matter," he mumbled.

'Then he spoke in a tone she had never heard since the days before their marriage, a cringing, whining tone.

'"Let me be, Ruth, my pretty little Ruth; I'm up to no

wrong, I promise you. Be kind to your poor Rawdon, darling," and he tried to kiss her.

'But instantly with his servility she regained her disdain of him. She pushed him roughly from her.

' "Get out then; don't bother me."

'He went, swiftly, thankfully.

'The furtiveness which she had already noticed clung to him; he slunk about like a Jew, watching her covertly, answering her, when she spoke, in his low, propitiatory voice. She had lost all fear of him now. She ordered him about in a peremptory way, and he obeyed her, sulkily, surlily, when she was not looking, but with obsequious alacrity when her eyes were on him. His chief desire seemed to be to get out of her sight, out of her company. He moved noiselessly about the house, seeking to conceal his presence; "pussy-footed," was the word she used. Their relations were entirely reversed. With the acquiescent philosophy of the poor, she had almost ceased to wonder at the new state of affairs thus mysteriously come about. She dated it from the day he had first taken to the attic, realising also that a great leap forward had been made from the hour of her midnight visit to his bedroom. He was an altered being. From time to time he tried to defy her, to reassert himself, but she held firm, and he slid back again to his cowed manner. She became aware that he was afraid of her, though the knowledge neither surprised nor startled her overmuch. She merely accepted it into her scheme of life. She was also perfectly prepared that one day he should break out, beat her, and reassume his authority as master of the house and of her person.

'This, then, was the position at Westmacotts' while I toiled at Ephesus and received with such wide-spaced regularity little packets of seed from Ruth. The situation developed rapidly at a date corresponding to the time when MacPherson fell ill with cholera. It was then three months

185

since Westmacott, by going to the attic, had made the first concession to his creeping cowardice. He was looking ill, Ruth told me; his eyes were bright, and she thought he slept badly at night. Her questioning him on this subject precipitated the crisis.

' "Rawdon, you're looking feverish."

' "Oh, no," he said nervously. They were at breakfast.

' "Ay, dad," said the eldest boy, "I heard you tossing about last night."

'Ruth turned on him with that bullying instinct that she could not control, and asked roughly,—

' "What do you mean by keeping the children awake?"

'He cowered away, and she went on, her voice rising,—

' "I won't have it, do you hear? If you can't sleep quietly here, you can go and sleep elsewhere – in the stable, for all I care."

'He didn't answer, he only watched her, huddled in his chair – yes, huddled, that tall, lithe figure – watched her with a sidelong glance of his almond eyes.

'She went on storming at him; she says she felt like a person speaking the words dictated to her by somebody else, and indeed you know Ruth well enough to know that this description doesn't tally with your impression of her.

'He was fingering a tea-spoon all the while, now looking down at it, now stealing that oblique glance at his wife, but never saying a word. She cried to him,—

' "Let that spoon alone, can't you?" and as she spoke she stretched out her hand to take it from him. He bent swiftly forward and snapped at her hand like a hungry wolf.

'The children screamed, and Ruth sprang to her feet. Rawdon was already on his feet, over in the corner, holding a chair, reversed, in front of him.

' "Don't you come near me," he gibbered, "don't you dare to come near me. You said you nearly stopped me once" – oh little seed sown ten years ago! – "but by Hell

186

you shan't do it again. I'll kill you first, ay, and all your children with you, cursed brats! how am I to know they're mine?" and a stream of foul language followed.

'Ruth had recovered herself, she stood on the other side of the room, with all her frightened children clinging round her.

'"I think you must be mad, Rawdon," she said, as coldly as she could.

'"And if I am," he cried, "who's driven me to it? Isn't it you? making my life a hell, spying on me, chasing me even to my bed at night, ready to pounce on me the moment you get a chance? Oh, you hate me, I know; it's that other man you want, you've had your fill of me. Oh, you false, lying vixen, you're just waiting till you can get me – catch me asleep, likely; what was you doing in my room that night? The woman who can shoot at a man once can shoot at him twice. Mad, you say I am? No, I'm not mad, but 'tis not your fault that I wasn't mad long ago."

'The eldest boy darted across the room at his father, but Rawdon warded him off with the chair.

'"Keep the brat off me!" he cried to Ruth. "I won't be answerable, I'll do him a mischief."

'He cried suddenly,—

'"This is what I'll do if you try to lay hands on me, you and all your brood."

'He was near the window, he took the pots of geranium one by one off the sill, crying, "This! and this! and this!" and flung them with all possible violence on the tiled floor, where the brittle terra-cotta smashed into fragments, and the plants rolled with a scattering of earth under the furniture.

'"I'll do that with your heads," he said savagely.

'His eye fell on the cage of mice, left standing exposed on the window-sill. At the sight of these his rage redoubled.

'"*He* gave you these," he shouted, and hurled the cage from him into the farthest corner of the room.

187

'He was left quivering in the midst of his devastation, quivering, panting, like some slim, wild animal at bay.

'The storm that had swept across him was too much for his nerves; the expression on his face changed; he sank down in the corner, letting the chair fall, and hiding his face in his hands.

' "There, it's over," he wailed, "don't be afraid, Ruth, I won't touch you. Only let me go away now; it's this life has done for me. I can't live with you. You can keep the children, you can keep the farm; I'm going away, right away, where you'll never hear of me again. Only let me go."

'It seemed to be his dominating idea.

'She moved across to him, but he leaped up and to one side before she could touch him.

' "Keep away!" he cried warningly.

'He reached the door; paused there one brief, intense moment.

' "You'll hear from me from London," he uttered.

'He seemed to her exactly like a swift animal, scared and untamed, checked for one instant in its flight.

' "I'll never trouble you more."

'Then he was gone; had he bounded away? had he flown? she could not have said, she could only remain pressed against the wall, the children crying, and her hands clasped over her heart.

'There, what do you think of that for the story of a Kentish farm-house? What a train of dynamite, isn't it, laid in the arena of Cadiz? What a heritage to transmit even to the third generation! You don't believe it? I thought you wouldn't. But it is true.

'Ruth told me the whole of this amazing story in a low voice, playing all the while with her two faded roses. She showed me a lawyer's letter which she had received next day, formalising the agreement about the farm, stipulating

188

that she should pay rent; all couched in cold, business-like terms. "Our client, Rawdon Westmacott, Esq.," that savage, half-crazed, screaming creature that had smashed the flower-pots only a week before. . . .

' "I see you've replaced the geraniums," I said rather irrelevantly.

' "Yes."

' "What about the mice?"

' "They all died."

'So that chapter was closed?

' "At any rate, Ruth, you need not worry now about your children."

'She looked puzzled.

' "Never mind, I was only joking."

'Then we were quite silent, faced with the future. I said slowly.

' "And you brought me down here to tell me all this?"

' "Yes. I am sorry if you are annoyed."

' "I am not annoyed, but it is late and I must go back to London to-night."

'She came a little closer to me, and my pulses began to race.

' "Why?"

' "Well, my dear, I can't stop here, can I?"

'She whispered,—

' "Why not?"

' "Because you're here alone, even the children are away."

' "Does that matter?" she said.

'A ray from the setting sun slanted in at the window, firing the red geraniums, and the canary incontinently began to sing.

' "You came here once," said Ruth, "and you asked me to go away and live with you. Do you remember?"

' "My dear," I said, "I have lived on that remembrance for the last ten years."

'I waited for her to speak again, but she remained silent, yet her meaning was clearer to me than the spoken word. We stood silent in the presence of her invitation and of my acquiescence. We stood in the warm, quiet kitchen, where all things glowed as in the splendour of a mellow sunset: the crimson flowers, the sinking fire, the rounded copper of utensils, the tiled floor rosy as a pippin. In the distance I heard the lowing of cattle, rich and melodious as the tones within the room. I saw and heard these English things, but, as a man who, looking into a mirror, beholds his own expected image in an unexpected setting, I had a sudden vision of ourselves, standing side by side on the deck of a ship that, to the music of many oars, glided majestically towards the land. We were in a broad gulf, fairer and more fruitful than the Gulf of Smyrna. The water lay serenely around us, heaving slightly, broken only by the passage of our vessel, and the voices of the rowers on the lower deck rose up in a cadenced volume of song as we came slowly into port.

'Ever yours,
'CHRISTOPHER MALORY.'